IN HIS CORNER

IN HIS CORNER

WILL THE REAL BILLY JOE PLEASE STAND

Joan Moore Lewis

Writers Club Press
San Jose New York Lincoln Shanghai

In His Corner
Will the Real Billy Joe Please Stand

Writers Club Press
an imprint of iUniverse.com, Inc.

For information address:
iUniverse.com, Inc.
5220 S 16th, Ste. 200
Lincoln, NE 68512
www.iuniverse.com

ISBN: 0-595-19942-9

Printed in the United States of America

To the Moores and the Huddlestons

There is so much good in the worst of us,
and so much bad in the best of us,
that it ill behooves any of us
to find fault with the rest of us.

—James Truslow Adams

Contents

Acknowledgements xi

Introduction xiii

Prologue xv

Billy Joe 1

Big Red 9

The Wedding 17

New Orleans 23

Downtown 29

Babe in the Woods 40

The Magic Mirror 47

Family Reunion 54

Biloxi 58

Grits, Eggs, and Chicken Pot Pie 68

Lawyers and Politicians 75

In His Corner 82

The Piano 91

Bowling Green 97

Vegas 102

Little Rock to Memphis 110

Dixie Mafia 119

The Big Diamond 124

Church 131

Merry Christmas 138

Dallas to Birmingham 143

The Rude Awakening 154

The Final Goodbye 167

Epilogue 175

About the Author 181

Acknowledgements

To my former English teacher, Mrs. Jimmie Cole, my heartfelt thanks for your encouragement.

To a good friend and former neighbor, Betsy Donovan, you were a godsend with your "free advice" and critique.

I appreciate the support of long-time friends and former co-workers: Colleen, Fran, Edie, Mary P., Earl, Elizabeth, Matt, Billy, Catherine, and Flossie B.

Introduction

Meet the characters in this story of friendship, love, loyalty, fun, adventure, and suspense.

Billy Joe Billingsley, a true Southern gentleman, was emotionally scarred from being sent to prison at age eighteen. Billy Joe yearned for his hometown but felt that he did not fit in after serving time. His life could never be the same.

Jane Moss, a small town, hard working, innocent Southern girl, who stayed busy trying to act worldly in the big city.

Harry Ledbetter, one of Billy Joe's associates, was a burglar, con man, and pimp. Jane thought Harry was a bad influence on Billy Joe.

Al Lawrence, an old and wise businessman, wanted what was best for Jane. He warned her about Billy Joe, his associates, and the so-called Dixie Mafia.

Lucky, Jane's good-hearted, supportive uncle, was caught up in the "seedy" side of life. He realized how hell-bent Jane could be.

Phoebe was Jane's best friend and advisor. A little older and a lot wiser, she was certainly more cosmopolitan than Jane.

Blanche, a switchboard operator by day and barmaid by night, knew almost everything. She was Jane's neighbor.

Prologue

"It was the 3rd of June, another sleepy, dusty Delta day…" That song, those words. The same song and words I heard in 1967—the first time he said, "I can't see you anymore."

The words still ring in my ears, "I'm bad; you're good. Neither one of us can change. Don't you understand?"

Bobbie Gentry's *Ode to Billie Joe* was a big hit in 1967. People who know the song remember the news from Choctaw Ridge—Billie Joe jumped off the Tallahatchie Bridge.

Over thirty years later, I drive into the churchyard next to the cemetery across from Billingsley Road, to visit the grave of William Joseph Billingsley—remembered by many who had known him as the notorious Billy Joe. He jumped off a bridge, too. Not literally, but with the same result.

When I was younger, I worried about what people thought. For several years, some people in Overton had treated me as though I was hiding a deep, dark secret. But it was no secret that Billy Joe had been my best friend; and I had been his. I just wouldn't allow myself to discuss it with anyone. Now I find it amazing, after all these years, how little I care about what people think.

Reaching over the seat, I pick up the flowers. The song is ending: "…And me, I spend a lot of time pickin' flowers up on Choctaw Ridge, and drop them into the muddy water off the Tallahatchie Bridge."

1.

Billy Joe

On a Friday night in the spring of 1967, I collided with Billy Joe Billingsley near the dance floor at Kitten's Korner on Peachtree. We turned, facing one another. He placed his hand on my arm and asked, "Are you okay?"

I looked at him in astonishment and blurted out, "Billy Joe, where in the world have you been?"

Now why did I ask that? Why couldn't I have said something clever? I had not seen Billy Joe since he left Overton, our hometown, and that had been over eleven years ago. I wished I had said something different—something more sophisticated.

He stood there looking puzzled. Then he started smiling. I had never seen a more handsome man. And he was still holding my arm. "Do I know you?" he asked. When I said I was Jane Moss from Overton, he remembered me. We had attended the same church.

As a seventh grader, sometimes I would see Billy Joe and his friends on the street when I walked from school to take piano lessons. I knew Billy Joe and most of his friends, but I didn't speak to them. I was only twelve, and they were in high school.

Billy Joe's mother had died soon after he was born. He lived in a big white house with his father, his older sister, and his Aunt Aggie. When Billy Joe was not in school or church, he was hanging out with his friends.

Once I saw Billy Joe at the county fair with his cronies from school. A few months after the county fair, he was with a group of young people from a neighboring town when they were taken into custody for some crime that had been committed. I thought it was for stealing hubcaps. I heard that his companions were sent to juvenile homes. Billy Joe had recently turned eighteen; he was sent to prison.

Some people called Billy Joe a juvenile delinquent. Others said Billy Joe was not a bad teenager, and that this would not have happened if he had been with his own circle of friends from school. They were all well-mannered boys from good homes, and while their behavior was usually prankish, they did nothing for which they should go to prison.

After serving time in prison, Billy Joe returned to Overton. One day I saw him standing in front of the pool room. At that time, he was a tall, gangly teenager wearing a brown suede jacket with a zip-up front. I was thirteen by then, and I thought he was cute.

He enrolled in school, but nothing was the same for him. His lifelong friends had graduated while Billy Joe was in prison. People said that Billy Joe felt he didn't fit in. He left Overton and was not seen again except when he visited his Aunt Aggie.

As a senior in high school, I wrote a term paper titled "Juvenile Delinquency." I thought about Billy Joe the entire time I was working on the paper. I wondered why some people had called him a juvenile delinquent. Nothing in my research pointed to a person like him. All the delinquents in the research were urban juveniles. They were not at all like Billy Joe. Those teenagers hung out on dirty streets in the big cities. Billy Joe had been a small town teenager who had loyal friends and attended church every Sunday. I wondered what had happened to him. I never dreamed I would see Billy Joe again.

That night, as we stood near the dance floor and chatted, I told Billy Joe I was there with my brother and two of his college friends who had driven over from Athens. They wanted a night out in Atlanta, and I had volunteered the use of my living room floor as their sleeping quarters for the night.

I learned from Billy Joe that he had been traveling during the past two years. I asked how his Aunt Aggie was doing. He told me she was overjoyed to have him back in the house after such a long time. His room was the same as he left it, and that's where he was staying while in Atlanta.

Billy Joe's father had remarried many years after the death of his mother. When Billy Joe's sister got married, his aunt built a smaller home. She always had a room for Billy Joe.

The music started again, and Billy Joe asked me to dance. When the music ended, he walked me to the table where I introduced him to my brother, Johnny, and his schoolmates. It was late, and Johnny asked if I was ready to leave. Billy Joe looked at me and said, "Why don't we go to a couple more places, and then I will take you home." That was fine with me. I gave the apartment key to my brother as we all walked out the door together.

Billy Joe escorted me to his car and opened the door. I surmised that he must be successful; he was driving a Cadillac Coupe de Ville and wearing a silk suit. Billy Joe was about 6'4" with jet-black hair, soft eyes, and the nicest smile I had ever seen. Being tall, distinguished and meticulously dressed made him stand out in a crowd. I wondered what kind of business he was in. He looked quite different from the everyday businessmen with whom I worked.

I was grateful that I had been out with my brother and his friends; otherwise, I would not be going anywhere with Billy Joe. While 1967 was the year of the hippies and the go-go clubs, it would not have been proper for a twenty-four-year-old young lady to be seen at a dance club without an escort. If my escort had been anyone other than my brother, it was improbable that I would be leaving with Billy Joe. That would not have been decent, and I was very conscious about what was decent and what wasn't.

We stopped by two after-hours clubs where a number of people knew Billy Joe, and they were all happy to see him. From their conversations, it was obvious they had not seen him in a long time. He introduced me to everyone he knew. He told a few of them that I was his "childhood sweetheart." I knew that was not true, but Billy Joe seemed to enjoy telling it. They were all friendly to me.

While Billy Joe was a quiet person, he was very polished and an excellent dancer. He had the manners of a Southern gentleman. When Billy Joe took me home, he walked me to the door and asked if I would have dinner with him the following night. I told him I would.

As I entered the apartment, I didn't even trip over Johnny and his two friends who were scattered across the living room floor sound asleep. I floated across them on "cloud nine."

I had dinner with Billy Joe the following night—and the next night—and the night after that. We dressed in casual clothes and ate in restaurants such as the Colonnade, located on Cheshire Bridge. I liked their salmon croquettes, and so did Billy Joe. We had barbecued ribs at the Hickory House on Piedmont, and shrimp at Crossroads where Peachtree met West Peachtree.

Sometimes, after dinner, Billy Joe would drive to Overton. After passing the city limits sign, he would make no more conversation. He would take the same route every time—past the high school; through the subdivision where his friend, Harley, lived; around the courthouse; and past Aunt Aggie's house. I could see that he was reminiscing by the expression on his face and the way his bottom teeth would bite into his upper lip. Leaving Overton, as he drove past the city limits sign headed north, he would reach over, pat my arm, turn up the volume on the radio and step on the gas pedal.

One night at dinner, I was telling Billy Joe about my day at work. Then I asked him where he worked. He said, "I do what everybody else does. I gamble. Don't you know that life's a gamble?"

I said, "What's your real job?"

He answered, "That is my real job. Gambling, and selling merchandise. You could call me a distributor."

After I learned that Billy Joe was a gambler, I was not surprised that he was acquainted with Lucky, the greatest uncle in the whole world.

Lucky had friends all over town, and he was also a gambler. I had been spoiled by Lucky, because I was his favorite niece. When I was a child, Lucky backed his car over my tricycle. He didn't buy me a new one, but he had been paying for it ever since. Lucky owned a bar and grill on the south side of town.

Billy Joe seemed to have plenty of money. He and I were constantly going places and doing things.

A week from the night we literally bumped into each other at Kitten's Korner, Billy Joe and I went dancing. We were leaving Whisk-A-Go-Go when I spotted Gregg coming in. I had gone out with Gregg some Saturday nights for the past two months. When Gregg had called to ask if I would like to go out on that particular night, I told him I would be in Overton for the weekend. He said, "Well, if you're going to be out of town, I'll catch you later."

Then he saw me with Billy Joe. As he walked by, he looked at me and said, "Out of town, eh?" He smirked at Billy Joe and kept walking.

As we stepped out the door onto the sidewalk, Billy Joe smiled and asked, "Friend of yours?"

I said, "Yes, he worked at my company during the summers when he was in college." Billy Joe kept smiling. There was a smile on my face, too. I was proud to be seen with Billy Joe.

I met several of Billy Joe's friends. Big Red was my favorite. He was a big and jovial bald-headed man who acted like a comic. He had the ability to make anyone laugh. Billy Joe told me that Big Red was a bookie.

One morning, we were meeting Big Red for breakfast at the Pancake House on Peachtree. Upon arrival, I noticed Big Red sitting in a booth with another man. Billy Joe said, "I see Harry made it."

So his name was Harry. Billy Joe introduced us. Harry was of medium build, with brown hair, and blue eyes. He had a serious, brooding look on his face. I sat there and wondered if he was a bookie, like Big Red, so I asked him what he did. Harry said, "You might say I'm in the entertainment business. My wife, Renee, is an exotic dancer." He said she had a booking that weekend. Those were the only words Harry spoke directly to me. He seemed to ignore me by excluding me from all other conversation, and that made me feel uncomfortable. I was happy when we finished breakfast.

Billy Joe was out of town most of the time. Sometimes, on weekends, he would call and ask me to catch a plane to the city where he was staying. He would pick me up at the airport, and we would have breakfast or lunch with his friends. Billy Joe had a wide variety of friends throughout the southeast. Then we would drive home together on Saturday or Sunday. We had lots of fun, just riding and talking.

One night after dinner, Billy Joe said that he and Harry had to go to Charlotte on business. He said he would leave his car with me if I could drive up the following Saturday morning and pick him up. Harry wouldn't be able to come home on Saturday, and Billy Joe didn't like to fly. I was tickled pink, but I tried to remain poised in Billy Joe's presence. I shrugged my shoulders nonchalantly when I said, "I guess I could." So he called Harry to pick him up. When Harry arrived, Billy Joe's car remained in my parking lot, and they left for Charlotte in Harry's car.

The next day I received a dozen red roses at the office. The card was signed "Love." That was the first of many dozens of red roses I would receive from Billy Joe when there was no occasion whatsoever. The cards were always signed, "Love."

On Saturday morning, I started out at 7:30, as Billy Joe had asked me to do. During the drive up, I wondered if Billy Joe was working with Harry in his entertainment business. Or perhaps he was in Charlotte gambling.

Billy Joe had given me his room number and directions to the motel near Charlotte. He had told me it would take four hours, if I didn't drive too fast. In exactly four hours, I drove up to the motel, and there stood Billy Joe on the second floor in front of his motel room. Laughing and pointing to his watch, he came down the stairs with his bags and placed them in the trunk. He said, "Good timing, Baby," as he got in the car.

I didn't inform him I had been fifteen minutes early and had stopped for coffee to kill time. He didn't need to know how fast I had driven.

Billy Joe said, "Let's stop somewhere and have lunch. I'm starving to death."

Billy Joe usually stopped at local restaurants when we were on the road. He said those were the ones that served the best food and that they usually served creamed potatoes. If creamed potatoes were on the lunch menu, then that's what Billy Joe ordered. Baked potatoes were his favorite at dinner, with butter, salt, and pepper. I had noticed that he was not particularly fond of sour cream, chives, or any of the other trimmings on his baked potatoes. But if they were served with all the extra trimmings, he never complained.

During lunch, he was in an easy-going mood and chatted away. As we were leaving, Billy Joe told me that he knew I must be tired of driving, so he would drive us home.

As soon as we were in the car, Billy Joe turned the radio dial to one of those "easy listening" stations. The music to *Mack the Knife* was playing. Billy Joe leaned over toward me and started singing the lyrics. When he got to the part, "Down by the river dontcha know," I joined in.

The song ended, and I said, "Billy Joe, I didn't know you could sing."

He replied, "I didn't either until today."

After that day, he would sometimes walk up to me in a store, lean over and whisper, "Down by the river dontcha know." When he did that, it would remind me of our trip from Charlotte, and I would inevitably start laughing aloud.

On the ride from Charlotte to Atlanta, Billy Joe asked me if I had seen anything interesting on the drive up. I couldn't remember anything in particular, except the freeway. When I told him that, he laughed and said, "Baby, you need to pay attention to detail."

I paid more attention to detail than Billy Joe would ever imagine. I didn't let him know I could fully describe the backside of a passenger seat in a Delta plane, and that I would recognize the windshield of his car anywhere!

I was frequently riding or flying somewhere. I had never had so much fun or felt so happy to be alive. It was not because I was traveling so much; it was because we were together.

2.

Big Red

He was called Big Red. I had only seen him a couple of times. When Billy Joe told me we were going up to Big Red's, I asked why he was called that. Billy Joe replied, "I guess it's because he drives that big red Cadillac convertible. But then, thinking back on it, I don't really know. He's always been called that—even when he drove a black car. Why are you constantly asking questions like this?"

"Well, I don't know," I said. "I could understand if he had red hair, but it just seems odd to call somebody Big Red when they're big and bald headed."

We were on our way up to Big Red's apartment on Roswell Road. Billy Joe had asked him if we could ride around in his convertible. It was such a pretty Saturday, and he thought we should do something nice on a pretty day. Sometimes Billy Joe had lots of nervous energy. Other times, he was real quiet and lifeless. Goodness knows we had spent enough time going to movies when he was in a quiet mood—seeing as many as three or four movies in one day.

Big Red greeted us at the door with a dishtowel in his hand. He said, "Give me a minute. I'm cleaning up the breakfast dishes."

Billy Joe and I sat in the living room. I noticed that Big Red had expensive furniture, and I didn't see a speck of dust anywhere. I had never been in a bookie's house before.

When he finished in the kitchen, Big Red walked into the living room and pointed to the wall behind the sofa. "I think a size less than 50 x 50, maybe a 43 x 43, would do nicely there, don't you?" he asked. "Let's run down to that new art place and see what they've got."

"I wouldn't know a Picasso from a Van Gogh," replied Billy Joe. "Take Jane. She has a good eye for things like that. I have to make some phone calls anyway."

"I heard that you have a photographic memory, Jane, so remember, no larger than a 50 x 50, okay?" said Big Red.

"She does have a good memory, if I could get her to pay attention to detail," laughed Billy Joe. "I don't know what's wrong with her. Either she's not interested, or she doesn't care. She just doesn't notice little things."

I didn't say a word. I would let Billy Joe think what he wanted to think. I paid more attention than he realized.

Big Red and I walked out to his car and drove down to the strip mall where a new art gallery had recently opened. We arrived there during the lunch period. Only one lady was working at that time, and she had several customers. We browsed for about thirty minutes, and Big Red measured a couple of the larger pieces. He would stand back and study each picture through his black framed glasses, as though he were an art critic. He found one painting he really liked, and I thought he was going to purchase it. When the after-lunch crowd started coming in, the place filled up. The lady was so busy that we left without talking to anyone.

When we arrived back at the apartment, Billy Joe was ready and raring to go riding in the convertible. The first thing he did was let the top down. My dark brown hair was fine and thin, and I complained about the way it was blowing all over my head. Billy Joe stopped at an accessories shop and found a red and black hat to match my red knit sweater, black pants, and sunglasses with black frames. Wearing a hat, I felt much better about riding with the top down.

We turned off Peachtree and headed west. Then he turned down a side street and told me we were going to look at townhouses. There was a man in a little house at the big gate who directed us to the office where a real estate agent was on duty. We went inside the office and met the lady. Her name was Mrs. Scott. After asking Billy Joe several questions and showing him floor plans and specifications, Mrs. Scott escorted us across the lawn to see one of the units.

Billy Joe asked questions about the construction and the materials used in the walls. He told her he was also interested in the overall security. She said, "We have excellent security. A guard is on duty from six o'clock in the morning until midnight, seven days a week."

We walked back to the office, and Mrs. Scott gave him more pricing information and asked how he planned to obtain his funds—would it be cash, or did he plan to finance? He told her he had an inheritance, but planned to leverage his money by financing a portion of the sales price. I wanted to ask him who died, but I didn't dare do it at that time.

She was pressing him for a phone number and address when he finally said, "I will go ahead and arrange for financing next week. Since I'm from out-of-state, I won't be back for two weeks, so I'll give you a call then." He took her card and we left.

When we reached the car, Billy Joe said, "Why didn't you say something? For somebody who's constantly talking, you were mighty quiet."

I replied, "I was speechless after learning that you had an inheritance. I was wondering who had died. I didn't know anybody in your family was even sick." He shook his head and laughed.

We returned the convertible to Big Red, thanked him, and went down to Lenox Mall. After we browsed a while and ate dinner, Billy Joe drove me home. He dropped me off at the door and didn't even bother to get out. He said he had things to do. After such a busy day, I was ready to be alone for a while anyway.

I slept until almost lunchtime on Sunday. When I finally got up, I made a pot of coffee and watched the noon news on television. The headline news was that there had been a burglary during the night at the same art store Big Red and I had visited. I wondered if Big Red had seen the news. I hoped they didn't take the painting he wanted.

Two weeks later, when Billy Joe came by on Friday evening, I asked him if we were going back to see Mrs. Scott at that fancy place with the man at the gate. He said, "No. I don't want to live there. While we were in Biloxi last weekend, somebody went into one of the vacant units after midnight, bored a hole through to the next unit and removed all the valuables of the people who live there. They were out of town, too. I can't live in that place, Baby. They don't have enough security."

Billy Joe walked over to the stereo and started playing a Sergio Mendes & Brasil '66 album; *Fool on the Hill* was one of his favorites. He turned, looked at me as he sat down, and said, "Besides, I need to go to Birmingham tomorrow. Why don't you go with me? You can drive."

"I'll go, but I'm not driving. The weatherman said it would rain all day. And I can't drive in the rain," I said.

"Why not? When you got your driver's license, did they tell you not to drive in the rain?"

"You know they didn't. I just can't drive in the rain."

"If you can't, you need to turn your license back in. You accepted that license under false pretense."

"But they didn't even mention driving in the rain," I said. "I just don't want to."

Billy Joe had a positive attitude. He said, "We'll see. The weatherman could be wrong."

It was early when Billy Joe came by for me the next morning. He opened my car door and then went around, got under the wheel and drove off. He had not even mentioned my driving. The only thing he said was, "I guess the weatherman was wrong." That was a true statement. It was a beautiful, sunny day.

Billy Joe was singing along with Otis Redding. When he wasn't tuned in to the "easy listening" stations, his radio dial was on the soul music and rhythm and blues stations. He enjoyed listening to Solomon Burke, Ben E. King, Arthur Conley, James Brown, Chuck Berry, Lou Rawls, and

Little Richard. Having friends who were owners of clubs, Billy Joe was acquainted with several entertainers from the south.

I was thinking of the South when, out of the clear blue, I asked, "Billy Joe, do you ever say 'fixin to?' I know you say it to me, but do you say it to other people?"

He replied, "Sometimes. It depends on the person I'm talking to. Why?"

"When I was working in Mr. Phillips' art studio last week, one of the commercial artists had a call from friends who asked him to lunch. He told them he was glad they called when they did—that his gofer had not gone out for his sandwich yet, but was 'fixin to.' He said I was always 'fixin to' do something. Damn Yankees! Why did they come down here anyway? We have artists in the South who can do ads in magazines and newspapers. And not only did he call me a 'gofer,' he ridiculed my Southern words! I've worked for attorneys and they never ridiculed anything I said. They all had a Southern accent, too. And they were proud of it. So am I. But I will never say 'fixin to' at work again."

Billy Joe patted my arm and said, "It's okay for you to say 'fixin to.'"

"I know you talk Southern to me, Billy Joe, but I've noticed that sometimes when you're speaking with other people, you don't even have a Southern accent. How do you do that?"

"As I said before, it depends on the person I'm talking to," said Billy Joe. "I can relax around you, and I talk Southern when I'm relaxed."

I replied, "Well, I'm not gonna relax around anybody but you, ever again, unless they're real Southern."

And Billy Joe was real Southern to me. Some people thought Southerners who had double names were "rednecks." Billy Joe was anything but a "redneck." I had never seen him wear a pair of jeans. I didn't even know if he owned any. He had worn expensive dress slacks and Bally shoes since I had known him. He didn't drive a truck; he didn't drink beer, and he rarely listened to country music. I had not heard him use profanity, and he could unerringly conjugate all of his verbs. Billy Joe knew the proper thing to do in any circumstance. I had never known anyone like him.

Billy Joe reached over, squeezed my hand, and said, "You worry too much about what people think, Baby." Maybe I did worry too much, but no matter what I worried about, I could discuss it with Billy Joe. Sometimes I would see the hint of a glimmer in his eyes as I asked a detailed question, and I would think he was amused that I worried so much about the least little thing. But, in his most solemn voice, Billy Joe would give me a clear and concise answer to any question I asked.

Before we reached Birmingham, Billy Joe told me he had to go to Victor Latimore's house and pick up a commission on a job he had set up for Victor. When we arrived at Victor's house, I stayed in the car. Billy Joe rang the doorbell. A tall dark-haired man answered the door. They went inside for about five minutes, and then Billy Joe came back to the car and handed me an envelope. He said, "Put this in your bag until we get home." I didn't even wonder what was in the envelope. He had given me envelopes before to hold for him.

As I closed my new handbag, I asked Billy Joe if he had noticed it was a new one. He said, "Yes, it looks new to me, and the clasp makes a noise when you close it. It's a lot smaller. How are you gonna get all your stuff in it?"

I told him about finding it on sale in one of the shops on Peachtree. "I was just browsing through there last Tuesday on my lunch hour when I saw it on sale for only $20.00, and I thought that was a good price for soft leather. Then on Wednesday, I was in there again, and the same bag was only $15.00. I told the sales clerk that I had paid $20.00 for the same bag the day before. She said she was sorry, but the $15.00 price started Wednesday."

Billy Joe said, "I guess you were a day early on that one."

"That's not the point, Billy Joe. I don't think I'll ever go in that store again. I think they cheated me out of $5.00. They have all this money and all these handbags, so what's a little $5.00 to them?" I rattled on and on about it.

Finally, Billy Joe looked at me and said, "I've got $5.00 in my pocket. I'll give it to you if you'll just hush."

When he started reaching in his pocket, I hushed. I was no longer infuriated with the store. Just telling Billy Joe about it made me feel better.

On the outskirts of Birmingham, we stopped at Verdo's Restaurant for lunch. A friendly, family-type atmosphere was obvious when we entered. A tall man came over, shook hands with Billy Joe, and told him how good it was to see him again. Billy Joe introduced me to Verdo, the owner.

Verdo suggested the Salisbury steak and creamed potatoes for lunch. Billy Joe told me that anything in that restaurant would be "tasty." He said that he stopped there every time he was in the area. He and his friends had been eating there for years.

After lunch, we headed home. Billy Joe had to circle the block because of the one-way sign. He laughed about the sign and told me that sometimes he felt like he was on a one-way, dead end street. "But you wouldn't know anything about that—you've never broken the law," he said.

"Yes, I have, Billy Joe. One time several of us stole a one-way sign at the Youth Center in Overton. That's where we hung out on weekends— dancing, playing ping-pong and pool. Somehow that sign ended up under my bed, and my sister found it and told Daddy. He was mad about it, and the next day, he turned it in to Milton Riggs, the deputy sheriff. Mother said that Daddy told Milton he found the sign where it should not have been. So I did break the law one time.

"No, it was more than one time. Speeding is breaking the law, and one day in front of the drug store, Milton Riggs told me that if I didn't slow that car down, he was going to tell Daddy. At the time, I was probably thinking, 'Take me to jail, but please don't tell my daddy.' They never gave tickets or took us to jail for anything. They just told our parents, and I thought that was a lot worse than going to jail."

Billy Joe laughed and said, "Well, I guess you're not the 'Miss Goody Two-Shoes' that I thought you were."

He reached over and patted my arm. Then he turned up the volume on the radio and started singing along with the music. I was thinking that Billy Joe's life would have been different if he had stayed out of the neighboring counties. Billy Joe was the only teenager from Overton who ever went to prison, that I could think of. If he had gotten into trouble in Overton, they would have just told his daddy, too. That's the way they handled teenagers then.

Overton was such a small town then that there was only one city policeman, and he went home at dark. The sheriff's department ran everything, day and night, and they knew everybody in the county. I was glad I had moved to Atlanta.

Billy Joe was still singing along with the radio. The trip to Birmingham had been fun, and I didn't understand why he always asked if I would like to go places. He probably had no idea that I would blindly follow him anywhere. That's something I could not have done in Overton. Milton Riggs would have told my daddy.

3.

The Wedding

Billy Joe and I were having the time of our lives. Everything was going fine between us until my sister starting planning her wedding. I guess that wedding brought about more pain than anything else in my life. It was the sole reason Billy Joe told me he couldn't see me anymore, and I thought it caused my family practically to disown me.

I had picked up the fabric for the dress I would wear in the wedding. Donna and I were on the phone talking about the dress pattern when she said, "I hope you don't think you're bringing him. Daddy would have a fit."

I asked, "Who?"

She said, "You know who, Billy Joe."

I proceeded to tell her that he had not been invited, and I questioned why she thought I would bring him anyway. She replied, "You know how you are."

I couldn't understand why she had brought up Billy Joe's name. I had informed Mother that I was seeing him, but I had no idea it would cause such turmoil. I knew Billy Joe's reputation in Overton was not a good one, only because he had made a mistake when he was younger. Surely, they wouldn't penalize him for the rest of his life because of one little mistake.

I told Donna that I would bring the fabric back to Mother's and she could do what she wanted to with it. I said, "I certainly don't plan to go to the wedding."

Later, when Billy Joe came to pick me up, I told him about the argument on the phone. I was so upset I could hardly talk. "Donna said to me, 'You know how you are.' No, I don't know. How am I? Tell me, Billy Joe, how am I?" I cried.

Billy Joe sat facing me on the sofa. He tried to calm me. I said, "They have disowned me. Why do they feel that way about you, Billy Joe?" I kept crying.

He said, "They didn't disown you, Baby. She didn't ask you not to go to the wedding; she just didn't want me there. If you stop seeing me, everything will be okay again."

My crying made Billy Joe restless. Then he told me it would be best for me and everyone concerned if he stopped seeing me. He said, "I don't want to cause you any more grief, and I know it will be like this from now on if I don't drop out of the picture. Believe me, it's for the best. The sooner I do it, the better it will be for you. They will never accept me, and you will never be happy as long as I'm around. This will not work out because of what I do. Don't you see? I'm bad; you're good. You can never be bad, and I can never be good. Neither one of us can change. Don't you understand?"

"You could change, Billy Joe. You could get a real job," I cried.

"Even if I did, it would not help this situation. Believe me, Baby, it's for the best." He kissed me on the forehead and quietly walked out the door. I had stopped crying, but I started again as the door closed.

A little later, there was a knock at the door. My first thought was that he had returned. I got up from the sofa, grabbed a tissue and dried my eyes. When I opened the door, there stood my neighbor, Blanche. I could tell from the stern look on her face that she already knew what had happened. She said, "I ran into Billy Joe in the parking lot."

I felt weak and thought I would faint. Blanche came over, put her arms around me and held me tightly and said, "Go freshen up your face. We're going out to eat." I had seen no one else argue with Blanche, so neither did I. Surprisingly, it was still daylight outside. I thought the whole world had turned dark. But it was only eight o'clock and would not be dark until after nine o'clock on this hot and humid summer evening.

It was a short drive from my apartment off Lenox Road to Mama Mia's Italian Restaurant on Peachtree near Tenth Street. We rode in silence. I was so choked up I couldn't talk. Blanche still had a stern look on her face. To know her is to love her. Blanche was a switchboard operator by day and a barmaid by night. Tonight was her night off.

Blanche had been my neighbor for almost a year and had taken on a big sister role. Kate, my next-door neighbor, had told me a little about Blanche's past. When Blanche was in her early twenties, she had met and married a Georgia Tech student from another country. For a few months, she was in wedded bliss. After his graduation from Tech, he returned to his country, leaving Blanche alone. A few months later, their son was born. She named him Perry.

Soon after Perry's birth, Blanche went back to work. She was working days in an office, and nights in a bar, struggling to make ends meet. Finally, Blanche was making enough money to be comfortable, but she was still working two or three nights a week as a barmaid. Perry was thirteen years old and no longer needed a baby sitter at night.

Even though I was miserable, I felt much better having Blanche take me under her wing. She was only thirteen years older than I, but Blanche was an all-knowing person. She did the talking at dinner. I was not hungry, but she insisted that I eat anyway.

Blanche talked about how people were so different, everybody needed somebody, what we wanted was not always what was best, how young I was, and she was sure I would forget in time. I just let her talk. I knew then that I would never forget.

Tears were pouring down my face as we sat in the darkened restaurant while Bobbie Gentry sang *Ode to Billie Joe*. That song made a lasting impression on me. We ordered a glass of wine. I could have drunk a whole bottle, but I remembered that Billy Joe always said,

"Don't drink too much, Baby. You need to pay attention to detail." So I only had one glass.

Blanche, with a concerned look on her face, was sitting across from me in the booth. Finally, she said, "He was right, Janie. One day you'll look back and see that he was right."

We got home before eleven o'clock. I went straight to bed and felt so exhausted that I fell asleep as soon as my head hit the pillow. The next day was Sunday and I moped around all day, thinking about Billy Joe.

It was a long and tiring week. I was unable to concentrate on anything at work. On Friday evening, arriving home from work, I could hear the phone ring as I unlocked the door. I answered, "Hello."

The abrupt tone of my voice seemed to say, "What do you want?"

After a long silence, the voice on the other end said, "Miss Moss? This is Billy Joe." As if I didn't know his voice! I had not heard from him since I told him about my sister's wedding, and that had been six days ago.

He said, "I've thought things over and I want you to know that I'm sorry about your sister's wedding, and I want to make it up to you. First of all, I want you to know I'm not taking responsibility for the fact that you will not be in the wedding and that you will not attend the wedding. That was your choice. But I do feel bad about the whole situation, since my name was brought up and caused you to lose your temper and make a stubborn, hard headed decision not to go.

"You know you and your sister never got along anyway, and if you couldn't use me as an excuse, you probably would have come up with something else. But then, on the other hand, I know how important it is for you to keep up appearances before God and all those folks in Overton. You can still go, you know. But now you're mad, and you're too embarrassed to back down after you told her what she could do with the fabric for your dress and the entire wedding. Enough said. Will you let me make it up to you as best I can?"

There was a long pause. He wasn't going to say anything else. He was waiting for an answer. Finally I answered, "I don't know."

"What do you mean, you don't know? After I gave you my long prepared speech, all you can say is 'I don't know?'"

"It's not that I don't know about you, Billy Joe, it's that I don't know what to do about my family," I said.

"There's one thing I learned a long time ago, Baby, and that is family will always take you back. You may not want to go, and they may not want you back, but no matter how many friends you have, you can only depend on family when the going gets tough. So you think about it. And while you're thinking, is it okay if I drive over and maybe we can go get a bite to eat or something?" he asked.

When Billy Joe arrived, he asked if I would like to have dinner downtown and go shopping. So we ended up at Davison's, and ate in the main dining room. After dinner, we looked at shoes for Tammy. Tammy was his daughter from a previous marriage. He and his ex-wife, Cheryl, were still friends, and Billy Joe could see Tammy whenever he was in town. Cheryl was not strict about his visitation.

There were so many different styles and colors that Billy Joe decided it would be a good idea to let Tammy select the shoes. He said Tammy had a mind of her own, and that he would pick her up one Saturday, and I could go shopping with them. We browsed a few minutes in the men's department, and then Billy Joe said, "Let's run down to Muses."

He was in the mood for clothes, so we rode down and parked near the C&S Bank Building and walked up to Muses. I liked Muses. In fact, two of my favorite dresses were from Muses. Billy Joe went straight to the men's department.

We were there until closing time. He purchased three suits, three ties, and three shirts. I could not believe the price! He charged these items and gave his father's address. He did not live with his father, so when we were walking back to the car, I asked him about it. He said it was okay because his father would pay for anything he purchased. "He's still on a guilt trip about the way he treated me when I was growing up. So I let him pay." I couldn't understand that, since Billy Joe always had enough money for anything he wanted.

After we got back to my apartment, I was making iced tea when I heard Billy Joe on the phone. He was saying, "Thought I'd let you know that I bought some new threads tonight. I'll mail you the money to pay the bill when it comes. Yeah, I'm okay."

Later, I walked back into the living room and said, "Billy Joe, did I just hear you call your father and tell him you would mail him the money for your clothes?"

He gave me a broad smile and said, "Yes, Baby, I don't want him to pay for anything I wear. I was trying to show you that you can go home again."

Sometimes Billy Joe went to a lot of trouble to "show me things."

4.

New Orleans

Billy Joe was taking me to New Orleans the weekend of my sister's wedding. He had stopped talking about "making it up to me," so that made it easier for both of us. I had Friday off so we would have time to drive. Billy Joe simply would not fly, and I was happy to be driving down with him.

On Friday morning, I was excited when I called Blanche at her job to let her know I was leaving for New Orleans. She said, "I'm glad you are going, but don't get too excited. I don't want you to be hurt again."

"Don't worry," I said. "If I die today, you can tell everybody I died a happy person. And I don't think I will ever be hurt by anyone again—not even Billy Joe."

As soon as Billy Joe arrived, he loaded my luggage into his car, and we were on our way.

We stayed in a town near Biloxi on Friday night and had dinner by candlelight at a small restaurant. The violinist came to our table and serenaded me with *Summertime*. I had never been so dazzled.

On Saturday, we stopped in Biloxi for lunch at a restaurant on the water. It was an old and dilapidated place, and fishing boats were docked at the pier nearby. Billy Joe told me those were shrimp boats and that the men were drying their nets. He said that many people in Biloxi made a living from shrimping. Some of the men were young, muscular, and well tanned. Others were old and weather beaten. I asked Billy Joe why such old men were on the boats. He said, "They're not that old. You're seeing years of hard work and hot sun etched on their faces."

After we were seated, Billy Joe asked me if I would like oysters on the half shell. I said, "Goodness, no, Billy Joe. I couldn't eat raw oysters." He just laughed and ordered a dozen.

The waitress brought a huge platter. He dipped an oyster into the sauce, placed it on a cracker, and said, "Look how easy this is." It didn't look so appetizing to me, as I watched him eat the oyster.

Then he dipped another smaller oyster into the sauce, placed it on a cracker, and said, "Let's see you do it. It's real easy if you have it on a cracker. Or would you rather have it without the cracker?" He was holding it toward my mouth, and I don't know how I did it, but I ate the oyster.

He looked me in the eye and said, "That's all—you can't have anymore."

I asked, "Why not?"

Billy Joe grinned and asked, "Would you like another oyster?"

I said, "Yes, please." Billy Joe was right; it had been easy to eat an oyster on a cracker, and I had actually enjoyed it.

The waitress removed the oyster platter and served our shrimp. When he finished eating, Billy Joe sat and looked through the glass walls at the water.

"Baby, I could look at these muddy waters all day. It reminds me of my life. Sometimes dark brown, and sometimes shimmering gold," said Billy Joe.

I thought about what he had said, and I replied, "Billy Joe, we could call you Muddy Waters, except that name has already been taken."

Billy Joe told me he liked two songs by Muddy Waters—*I Can't Be Satisfied* and *I Feel Like Going Home*. He said that some people thought Muddy Waters was a blues man from Chicago, but he knew that Muddy Waters had been born right there in Mississippi, and that's how he got the name "Muddy Waters." I thought he was just kidding me again, but I could call Directory Service at the Atlanta Public Library and find out for sure as soon as I was back in the office. Mr. Green, my new boss, had said that I was resourceful and often asked me to check information for him.

After lunch, we drove along the sun-drenched beaches down what Billy Joe called, "The Strip." It looked cheap and gaudy to me, and I detested gaudy. Billy Joe told me his friends owned most of those clubs, but that "The Strip" was no place for me. He said, "It's illegal to buy a drink here, and gambling is illegal, too, but that's how a lot of people make a living in Biloxi."

When we arrived in New Orleans, we checked into the Prince Conti. I did not mention it to Billy Joe, but I was not impressed with all the old antique furniture; it made the room look dark. When Billy Joe opened the curtains, there was a glass door to the balcony overlooking Conti, and we could see Bourbon Street. He said, "Let's go take a walk." So we walked down Bourbon Street, window shopping and going in some of the small shops.

Billy Joe saw a black-and-white mini dress in one of the windows. We went inside to take a closer look. I tried the dress on, and he liked it because it was black-and-white, his favorite color combination. When I came out of the dressing room, he was at the cash register getting his receipt.

Back on Bourbon Street, there was music in the air – jazz, Dixieland, saxophone, and other sounds I couldn't identify. We stopped in Pat O'Brien's and had a Hurricane. I kept both glasses as souvenirs. There was a photographer who took our picture and told Billy Joe that he would have two copies delivered to the hotel the next morning. Billy Joe paid him and we left.

That evening, we dined at the Court of Two Sisters. Billy Joe suggested turtle soup and lobster étouffée, but I told him I couldn't eat that much. He said, "Baby, fine dining is an experience. You don't have to clean your plate. Just sample food you haven't eaten before. Now won't that be fun?"

He asked me if I had ever eaten an artichoke. I answered, "No, have you?"

"Yes," replied Billy Joe, "and when we get back to Atlanta, I will take you to the Coach and Six where they serve excellent artichokes." I wondered if that would be fun.

My red dress from Franklin Simon's was perfect for this festive evening. We went to Al Hirt's Place to see Fats Domino. There was a long line, but Billy Joe walked up to the door, gave his name, and they ushered us down to a front table. Billy Joe told me that he had lost his good watch to Fats Domino in a poker game a while back. And sure enough, Fats Domino, in person, said that he had special guests there that night. He looked at Billy Joe, held the arm that wore a handsome gold watch in the air and waved it three times. Then he laughed and started singing *Ain't That a Shame*. Billy Joe sat back in his chair and chuckled. I wondered if he was kidding me again, but I didn't think the Atlanta Public Library would know about a poker game.

It was late Sunday morning when I finally turned over and opened my eyes. The sun was shining through the glass door. Billy Joe was sitting at the small table drinking a cup of coffee. He looked over at me and said, "Sleeping Beauty! You don't need to drink Hurricanes. I thought you would never wake up."

He handed me the cup of coffee he was drinking. He told me this was the third cup he had brought me, and he thought he would have to drink it, too. He said, "I ate breakfast the second time out. I had a feeling it would be time for lunch before you could get dressed."

I said, "Why didn't you wake me up, Billy Joe?" He looked at me knowingly and shook his head.

I carried the coffee to the bathroom and started getting dressed. It was about an hour before I was finally presentable. Billy Joe had gathered our belongings and had the bags packed and waiting at the door. He was ready to go. When the bellhop arrived, Billy Joe asked him to hold our luggage downstairs until we returned from lunch.

We got on the elevator, rode down to the first floor, and stopped at the front desk. Billy Joe checked out and told them we would be back for the luggage in about an hour. Then we walked out the front door onto the sidewalk. Billy Joe said it was just a few blocks to a courtyard where we would have lunch.

After we had walked a short distance, Billy Joe reached over and opened a wrought iron gate. There was a large two-story house on the lot and I thought we were entering somebody's back yard. To my surprise, there were tables with white linen tablecloths in that yard. It was a restaurant! As soon as we were seated, a waiter brought water and menus.

I was thirsty. I picked up the water glass and started drinking. Billy Joe said, "Whoa!" He placed his hand around my hand holding the glass and gently set the glass on the table.

Then he said, "Go slow on that water. You had too many Hurricanes last night. I don't want you throwing up." I was still thirsty, but I didn't dare touch the water again.

Billy Joe suggested an oyster Po-Boy for lunch. I said, "Are you kidding? I've had a potato salad sandwich when there was nothing else in the refrigerator. But an oyster sandwich? I've never heard of such!"

He said, "Trust me, you'll like it."

The waiter brought the Po-Boy sandwiches, and I was surprised at how good an oyster sandwich could be. It was filled with small, soft-fried oysters. I couldn't identify all the ingredients in the sauce, but I could tell it contained some catsup and horseradish.

I said, "That was real good, Billy Joe. It made me thirsty. Now can I drink some more water?"

He replied, "Just a little. We'll get you some more later."

We walked back to the Prince Conti. The bellboy saw us enter the front door. He hurried over and said he would meet us at the side entrance to the garage with the luggage.

As we drove off, Billy Joe said, "This weekend has been a vacation to me. It's been a long time since I've had a real vacation." He reached over and squeezed my hand.

On the way out of New Orleans, he stopped and bought me a Coke. Then he went to the trunk and took a big manila envelope out of his luggage. He handed the envelope to me as he got in the car. I opened it, and there were two 8x10 photographs of us sitting in Pat O'Brien's. He said, "One for you, and one for me. I'm taking mine down to Aunt Aggie's. It will always be one of my prized possessions."

We started the long drive home. He turned on the radio and tuned in to one of the "blues" stations. We were both in a relaxed mood. Billy Joe was so attentive that it would have been difficult for me to feel otherwise. It had been a real vacation for me, too.

On the way home, I thought about our photo being one of Billy Joe's "prized possessions." One evening as we rode through Overton, Billy Joe had stopped at Aunt Aggie's. We sat in the living room and chatted with her a while, then Billy Joe stood up and said to me, "Come in here. I want to show you something."

I followed him into his room where he reached in his closet and removed a big brown box. He set it on the bed and said, "There are some things in here I want you to see—my prized possessions."

I was moved by the momentous items in the box, some of them dating back to his childhood. The story of Billy Joe's life was in that brown box. I felt as though he had shown me the core of his existence. Neither one of us mentioned the contents of the box after that day.

The New Orleans blues was still playing on the radio. As he drove, I reached toward him, and he placed his hand in mine.

5.

Downtown

I was in my heyday. Working and living downtown was exciting to me. Happy about life in general, I was thinking back on how it all had happened so fast.

I had worked for Mr. Phillips for six years. One time I had the silly notion to do something different. Mac, a sales representative for Mr. Phillips, left the company to open his own business, and he asked me to go with him. When I told Mr. Phillips I was resigning, he arched his eyebrow. I had seen him do that previously, and it was not the arch of the eyebrow that concerned me—it was the expression on his face that accompanied the arch.

After a few months of working with Mac, I was disappointed. He was nothing compared to Mr. Phillips. Mac didn't even know what the word "organized" meant.

I had thought the grass would be greener with Mac. When I discovered what a terrible mistake I had made, I phoned Mr. Phillips. He was very understanding, and he said he would be pleased to have me back.

I didn't go back to the same position as his executive assistant, however. Mr. Phillips owned two other offices in town, and he said he really needed me in both of those. Two or three days a week, I worked in his art studio. That job required me to call on customers, make notes of their revisions to artwork, and handle miscellaneous office duties. The remainder of the week, I drove to Phillips Research in Buckhead. There I sorted through files, photos, and artwork. Mr. Phillips called it "market research." An older lady came in two afternoons a week to help.

I felt isolated when she was not there. The work itself was not enjoyable at all.

I missed the camaraderie of the staff at Mr. Phillips' printing company. I remembered one time while working there that Mr. Phillips had handed me pages of a customer's camera-ready copy. He asked me to take it to typesetting and let them know that the headings and text were not compatible, and the headings needed to be changed. I walked into the typesetting department and said, "Here's some copy that needs to be fixed. Mr. Phillips said that it's not up to snuff."

Mr. Phillips had just walked in the other door to the department. Browning, one of the typesetters, looked at him and asked, "Did you really say that this copy was not 'up to snuff?'"

Mr. Phillips smiled and replied, "Something like that."

Mr. Phillips was a Yankee, but he could interpret my Southern words. The bottom line was that I got the point across, and there were never any misunderstandings as to what he had said. When I gave instructions to anyone in the company, they considered it "out of the horse's mouth." And Mr. Phillips had always stood behind any instructions I gave them. I realized that my job was to deliver the message. I didn't have to tell them how to do their jobs. They were the best in the business, and they knew what was needed.

It was obvious to Mr. Phillips that I was bored and unhappy with his "market research." One Friday, I found an envelope on my typewriter. It read: "Jane, I am enclosing your check for this week plus pay for an additional two weeks. During the next two weeks, please try to find something you really like." It was signed "M. Phillips." There was a P. S. that read "If you don't find anything, give me a call."

I was astounded! Mr. Phillips thought more about how I felt than he did his work. I was so relieved to be leaving that "market research" office. And it was Mr. Phillips' idea. He knew I would never make a decision to leave him twice, since I had learned my lesson about green grass.

My neighbor, Kate, was on vacation. On Sunday, I took her paper from the porch and looked in the classified ads. It was after nine o'clock Monday morning when I started calling the ads I had checked. The first phone call was to a Mr. Green who had advertised for an Executive Assistant. A man's voice answered. I asked for Mr. Green. To my surprise, it was Mr. Green who had answered the phone. I told him I was Jane Moss, and I was calling in response to his ad in yesterday's paper. He asked me a few questions, then he asked if I could come in for an interview around 11:30. I told him I could. The building was located downtown in Peachtree Center.

As I drove down Peachtree Street, I thought of Billy Joe and how he would drive down Peachtree every night we were together. It was the last thing he did before taking me home. Billy Joe called it a "ritual." Billy Joe also said, "Atlanta is the best city of all," and he had been in lots of cities.

I also thought of Billy Joe's drives through Overton. He never mentioned where we were headed, and he would always go at dusk and take the same route through town. On his way back to Atlanta, as soon as he passed the Overton city limits sign, he would pat me on the arm, turn up the radio volume and step on the gas pedal. Billy Joe had never said that driving through Overton was a "ritual," but I could tell that it was.

When I reached the building in Peachtree Center, I left my car with the garage attendant and walked to the front of the building. After entering through the revolving doors, I boarded the elevator to Mr. Green's floor. At the door to his suite, I took a deep breath and walked in. Mr. Green heard the door open and came out of his office. He shook my hand and said, "Jane, I'm Hiram Green. It's good to see you. I'm happy you could stop by today. Why don't we walk over to Stouffer's and have lunch?"

I said, "Thank you, I would like that."

During lunch, I observed Mr. Green's mannerisms and noticed that he had short, stubby fingers. He was not a tall man, and his hair was completely white. I guessed his age to be around fifty. I found myself comparing him with Mr. Phillips who was at least ten years younger. Mr. Phillips was tall and handsome, and he reminded me of a typical bank president. They both dressed in suits similar to those on display in the haberdasheries around town.

After Mr. Green explained the duties and responsibilities of the job, he asked me several questions concerning my capabilities. I must have given the right answers, because as soon as we finished dessert, he wanted to know how soon I could start work. I told him I could start the following Monday. He said, "Then, Jane, let's go back by the office so I can give you a key, in case you get there first on Monday."

I was elated to know I would have more money coming in for my bills—even more than Mr. Phillips had been paying me!

When Billy Joe was out of town, he would call me three or four times a week—sometimes at home, sometimes at work. He didn't talk long. I was glad he stayed out of town; that made it easier for me to concentrate on my new job, even though the job was an easy one. Mr. Green was usually out of town, except for Mondays.

Several of my friends worked downtown, so I had lunch buddies there. When I didn't have plans with them, I would walk over to the deli and get a chopped liver sandwich on an onion roll with a pickle and Coke. Then I would take it back to the office. One day I stepped into the door of the deli and stood in line to order my usual sandwich.

Al Lawrence, the owner of a nearby print shop, was standing next to me in line. I had met Al while working with Mr. Phillips and had seen him a number of times when I worked with Mac. He and his wife were fifty years old, or older. They both worked in town and lived in the suburbs.

Al said, "Hi, Janie. I haven't seen you in quite a while. It's good to see you, especially today. I need to ask you to do me a favor, if you will."

I said, "I'll be happy to, Al. What do you need?"

He said, "You know how I usually write out my invoices? Well, I've got a big one this week that I need to send out so I can get my money. I was wondering if you had time to come by and type it for me?"

I replied, "How about now? I can take my sandwich down there and eat while I'm doing the invoice. It won't take long."

Al smiled and said, "I'd be mighty obliged." When our take-out food was ready, we walked down the street to his shop. Things were really in a mess. Dust was everywhere, and he wasn't sure the typewriter worked. Fortunately, it did. I zipped out that invoice so fast he couldn't believe it.

Al said, "Boy, I wish I could get you to do all my invoicing. This really looks good."

"No problem, Al," I replied. "Why don't you just start making a list of who to, how much, and what for? I'll drop by once a week and get them out for you."

Al had a pleased look on his face when he said, "I can do my part, if you're sure you don't mind." That's when I started making extra money. I didn't think it would be a great deal, but in two weeks, Al was paying me as much in a few lunch hours as Mr. Green paid me for a whole week. I told him he was paying me too much, but Al insisted that since I had doubled his income by getting the invoices out so fast, he should be paying me for it. I wondered how much money Al had lost because he never got around to sending an invoice.

One day, I said, "Al, you can hire someone full time for what you're paying me."

He replied, "I don't want some woman here all day getting on my nerves. I like things the way they are." I liked things the way they were, too.

Thankful to be making extra money, I thought about my apartment lease being up at the end of the month. I had not signed a new lease, and I didn't intend to sign one. I wanted to move. Maybe if I moved, I would never be late for work again. As soon as I got home from work on a hot Monday afternoon, I checked the paper for apartments in the downtown area. I found one in a building downtown, a few blocks from Peachtree Center.

It was early Tuesday morning when I phoned the number in the ad. Mrs. Atwood, the leasing manager, asked if I would like to see the apartment that day. I told her I could be there on my lunch hour.

Driving up Peachtree, I located the building and turned into the parking lot. The banner read, "Now Leasing." The minute I walked into the lobby, I felt that this was the place for me. The marble floors were shiny, and there was a fresh cut flower arrangement on a table in the lobby. Mrs. Atwood showed me one of the apartments. Of course the rent was twice what I was paying, but my new salary and the money Al paid me for doing his invoicing would cover it.

I tried to weigh the pros and cons. My best friend, Phoebe, had said, "Change for the better doesn't come without compromise." Now what would I be compromising? I couldn't think of a thing. I signed the lease. I told Mrs. Atwood that I would like to move in on Saturday because of my work schedule. She said that they usually required tenants to move on weekdays, but in my case, she could allow me to move in the following Saturday.

I was ecstatic! I went back to work, called my leasing office, and told them I would be moving. Then I called to make arrangements with the movers.

I phoned Mr. Phillips to tell him the good news. He didn't sound excited. He said, "Do you think it's a good idea to make so many changes in just weeks, Jane?" I told him I thought it was a good decision, but after hanging up the phone, I started having doubts. Mr. Phillips had a tendency to make me think things through. Unfortunately, too many times, it was after the fact.

Billy Joe called Wednesday night. I informed him I was moving downtown and that I had already signed the lease. I remembered that when Mr. Green had suggested I move downtown to be near the office, Billy Joe was not too excited about the idea. But I didn't realize he would be opposed to it. He said, "Baby, now why would you want to go and do a thing like that?"

I told Billy Joe that he knew I was planning to move as soon as the lease was up at the end of the month. He said, "Yes, but I thought you would look around. Are you sure you can handle that high rent? And why do you want to move downtown? Why didn't you discuss it with somebody before you signed that lease?"

I said, "I discussed it with Lucky last night, and Lucky said, 'What in the hell is wrong with where you are now? You can do some of the most dumb-ass things.' But I told Lucky I was late for work sometimes because of the traffic, and that I wanted to move downtown because I wanted to drop my garbage down a chute instead of having to take it to the dumpster at the end of the parking lot.

"Lucky finally said, 'Well, if you're so hell-bent and determined, do what you want to do; that's what you're gonna do anyway.'" Billy Joe didn't say anything else about it, after I told him what Lucky had said.

Billy Joe should have remembered one of the reasons I wanted to get out of that apartment was because of the landlady, Mrs. Forrester. I knew I would never forget that incident. I had purchased drapes, sheers and traverse rods at J. C. Penney's. The sheers were easy to hang, but I had postponed hanging the drapes. Billy Joe had asked me what was in those bags on the bedroom floor. I told him drapes for the living room and dining room, but that I had to figure out how I was going to get them up. He said that was no problem. One day while I was at work, he installed the rods and put the drapes up.

When I got home from work that afternoon, I opened the door to the apartment. Billy Joe got up from the sofa to greet me. There was a big smile on his face. On the dining room table was a vase of cut flowers. The apartment was immaculate. I said, "Oh, Billy Joe, these flowers are beautiful. They look so fresh—as if you've just picked them."

He replied, "Well, I did." Then he told me about going to the store. While riding through one of the neighborhoods near North Druid Hills Road, he saw a man working in his garden where there were flowers of all colors and sizes. Billy Joe stopped and asked the man if he could buy a bouquet. The man said, "My flowers are not for sale, young fellow. Pick what you want." He picked a few dahlias and zinnias, and they made the perfect bouquet. Billy Joe said he had to stay for fifteen minutes and listen to the man talk about how he grew them.

Then Billy Joe told me that when he finished with the drapes, he sat down on the sofa to watch television. He kept glancing at the wax build-up on the kitchen linoleum. The apartment building was ten years old, and it looked as if that floor had not been thoroughly cleaned in ten years. Finally he could stand it no longer. That's when he went to the store on North Druid Hills for a new mop, floor cleaner and Mop and Glo.

When he returned from the store, he realized what a messy job cleaning that floor would be, and he didn't want to ruin his clothes. He took off his pants and shirt before he got down on the floor and cleaned it. He vacuumed the debris from drilling holes for the traverse rod, and he cleaned the front grill on the refrigerator. Then he used Mop and Glo on the kitchen floor.

Before he placed the vacuum cleaner back in the closet, he vacuumed the powder blue rug in the bedroom. He was down on his hands and knees, still in his briefs, taking boxes from under the bed so he could vacuum there when he felt a presence in the room. He said, "I looked up and there was this little lady pouncing on me like a banty hen."

Billy Joe told me that she was standing over him shaking her finger in his face. To complicate matters, there was all that noise from the GE canister vacuum cleaner. He couldn't understand a word she was saying, and he couldn't even reach the switch to turn the vacuum noise off. He said he looked to see if she had a gun in the other hand. Billy Joe was afraid of guns. He said that when a person had a gun, somebody always got hurt, and she definitely had him at a disadvantage.

He shouted above the noise, "Lady, who are you and what do you want?"

She told him she was Mrs. Forrester, the landlady, and it was against the law for Miss Moss to have a man in her apartment. He said, "She even threatened to have you evicted."

Still in the floor, on his hands and knees, Billy Joe said to her, "Lady, I don't think it's against the law for me to be here. She's not harboring a fugitive or anything. I'm not wanted anywhere for anything that I'm aware of. I suggest you either call the police or leave. You can use the phone in here; the kitchen floor is still wet."

As he got up from the floor, he said, "Now would you excuse me while I put on my pants? Don't look at me like that. A lot of men do housework in their underwear. And do you make it a habit of going around using that master key and barging in on half-naked men?"

He said she backed out the door, still shaking her index finger at him. When he finished with the vacuum cleaner, he took a shower and put back on his clothes.

He was still thinking about what Mrs. Forrester had said, so he called his attorney, Arthur Wallace, and asked him if there was such a law. Arthur told him that there had been one on the books over fifty years ago stating that it was unlawful for an unmarried woman to be in the room with a man. Arthur told him that there were a lot of those old ridiculous laws still on the books, but he had not heard of that one being enforced in the thirty-five years he had been practicing.

We met Big Red at the Hickory House for ribs that night. Billy Joe told Big Red about his incident with my landlady, and after he finally stopped laughing, Big Red said, "Of all the strange things that have happened to you throughout the years, I think this one just about tops them all."

Billy Joe said, "Well there's one thing for sure. You can't add this one to your list of funny stories. I don't want people to know I was doing housework. What would that do to my image?" He looked at me and winked.

On the way home from the Hickory House, I was thinking about how the laws discriminated against women. I told Billy Joe that I had decided to join the National Organization for Women. It was a new organization, and they had started sending me newsletters, probably because I had a subscription to the new *MS Magazine*. I told him that NOW wanted my membership dues, and the Republicans wanted my vote.

I said, "One day women won't be discriminated against like we are today."

Billy Joe reached over, patted my arm and said, "I know what you mean, Baby."

I wondered if he really knew. At the time, I just didn't see any hope for women. I could only see a man's world. It had always been that way, at home and at work. As long as men controlled the money, they would control the women. I decided that night to start saving more money.

Thursday and Friday went by in a hurry. I packed everything I owned and was ready for the movers on Saturday morning. It didn't take long for them to load the van, and we were on our way. I left the key to the old apartment in an envelope on the kitchen counter.

As I followed the movers, I wondered how my furniture would look in the new place. I had been on a buying spree the previous year and had purchased new furniture for the living room and dining room. I spent more than I had intended to spend on furniture, thanks to Dave McNabb.

Dave and his family owned a furniture store in Overton. One Saturday, Mother and I were in the store looking at the furniture. I couldn't find a thing I really liked. That's when Dave said, "Don't worry. You can run down to Southeast Wholesale and find anything you're looking for there."

The following week, I called Dave and set up an appointment to meet him the next morning at Southeast Wholesale. I saw the fruitwood, and I knew it was what I wanted. Dave knew it, too. I told him I didn't think I should spend that much, but again, he said, "Don't worry. You can pay a little each month."

I was happy with my selection of a dining table, four chairs, coffee table, end tables, and an emerald green sofa. If Dave was not worried about my paying him, then I wouldn't worry either.

Dave was a friend of the family. We had lived next door to him when I was in elementary school. Mother attended his wedding. It was a big occasion at the Baptist Church. Mother wore a new outfit—dress, hat, and shoes. A large photo of the bride had been in the Overton paper. She was a beautiful, slender brunette, and every person in town who knew her thought Dave had picked the right one. Dave told everybody that she was the one who did the "picking."

I would check with Dave to see if he had a rug for the living room in the new apartment. The floor throughout was parquet, and I would need a large accent rug. The only rug I owned was that powder blue rug in the bedroom. It was a gift from the advertising crew at Callaway Mills. I had helped organize the photography for a brochure of their products when I was working with Mac. They told me to pick out any rug I wanted. Why I chose that powder blue, I would never know.

I was glad Blanche was at work when I moved. She was quite upset about the whole situation when she found out I was moving. She said, "You can't fly so high so fast, Janie. You need to stay here longer, get adjusted to your new job, and then consider moving. You certainly don't need to live downtown. You need to be here, near your friends." I realized she was right, but I had already made decisions and signed papers.

Phoebe had been shocked at my decision, too. Even though she was my best friend, she said, "Well, you've always made rash decisions. You can do what you feel is best, but I hope you don't live to regret it."

Why did Blanche, Mr. Phillips, Phoebe, Lucky and Billy Joe all feel the same way? I had always been one to act first, and think later. I thought that having a new job and a new apartment would give me a new life. Little did I know.

6.

Babe in the Woods

The new Regency Hyatt House had opened, and Harry and Renee were waiting for Billy Joe and me in the lobby on a Friday night. We were having dinner together. I had already met Harry on the morning we had breakfast with Big Red, but I had not met his wife, Renee. She was petite, olive-skinned, and had long black hair and fiery eyes. I thought she had tons of cosmetics on her face, but upon closer observation, I could see that her complexion was the color of honey. I knew that she was an exotic dancer, but I wasn't expecting this. Billy Joe told me later that Renee was French Cajun from Louisiana.

After Renee and I were introduced, Harry said, "Tony and Eve are meeting us here. I hope that's okay." Billy Joe replied, "Fine, fine." When Billy Joe did a double word like that, I knew that either he was not listening or he was not happy.

Then they appeared. Tony had on a sharp suit, even sharper than Billy Joe's. He was not very tall, and he had dark hair and eyes. There was a sweet look on his face. Eve was tall and elegant, and she reminded me of how I thought a Greek goddess should look. She was stunning.

Our reservations were in the main dining room. I was hoping we would go up to the revolving bar, but the place was packed and the elevators were full. I was thankful Billy Joe and I had previously eaten at the coffee shop in the lobby; otherwise I would have felt like some of the sightseers who were staring upwards with mouths open. It was a 23-story atrium hotel with glass elevators in the center of the lobby. A person could ride the elevators and see each floor's balcony plus all the greenery and fine furnishings. I had never seen anything like it. But I didn't gawk—I acted as if I had been there many times.

After we were seated, I noticed the others were talking, but Billy Joe was quiet. I didn't say a word. I felt like a "plain Jane." Renee wore a kelly green and taupe dress with antique bangles and dangling earrings. Eve had on a pale green silk dress, with a V-neck, and it showed a lot of cleavage. Her jewelry was simple.

I had on the same outfit I had worn to work that day—a black and white checked knit from Joseph's. I was glad I had not worn one that I made. My earrings were the black coral studs that Mr. Green brought me from Hawaii, and I wore my watch and ring.

Tony was a fast talker, so I thought he could possibly be a salesman. I laughed softly at all the right places. I could tell, because Billy Joe would sometimes reach over and squeeze my hand. He had relaxed somewhat, and I thought everything was going well that evening.

After dinner, Tony said, "Why don't we go hit a few night spots? How about it, Billy Joe?" Billy Joe told him his back was aching so he thought we would call it a night. I was glad to be going home.

When we got to my place, Billy Joe said he wasn't good company. He said his back was still hurting, so he thought he would go. He hugged me at the door and said, "I have some things to do tomorrow, so I'll see you Sunday, Baby."

As soon as he left, I called Phoebe. She and I made plans to go shopping and have dinner at Lenox on Saturday. Phoebe and I had been best friends for six years. I met her when I first moved to Atlanta and was working in Calhoun Johnson's law office in a building near the Commerce Club and attending business school at night. Phoebe befriended me on my first day at work while we were standing in line at the downstairs coffee shop. She was petite with dark auburn hair. The first time I saw her, she was wearing a red three-quarter coat with black ribbing at the wrists and around the collar. The sleeves were pushed up halfway to her elbows. She looked sophisticated.

Phoebe and I had everything in common. We would shop and have dinner. Then we would go to her apartment on Peachtree near Piedmont Hospital and watch the Late Show on television while we sewed. She's the one who suggested I use Vogue patterns because they had more style.

During dinner Saturday night, I told Phoebe how uncomfortable I felt being around Harry. I asked her what a "babe in the woods" meant. She told me it was a person who was innocent, one who had not been around. I told her that the first time I met Harry, I didn't like him. When I talked, he would say under his breath, "a babe in the woods." Then he would roll his eyes and lean his head backwards. I said, "Last night I was very careful and just talked about the ferns or made one-sentence comments. Then they would make comments, so I wasn't required to say much."

I asked Phoebe if I was a "babe in the woods" when she met me six years ago.

She smiled and replied, "Yes, I believe you were."

On Sunday, Billy Joe called and asked if I would like to go see *Alfie* at one of the small theaters. We went, but it was not the best thing for his back. He called Tony from the lobby and asked if they had a heating pad. We stopped by to pick it up. Tony and Eve lived in a high-rise in Buckhead. Billy Joe gave me the apartment number and asked me to run up and get the heating pad. His back was really hurting after sitting at the movie.

I found the number and rang the doorbell. Eve came to the door. She looked quite different wearing shorts and a knit shirt. Her dark brown hair had been in an upsweep Friday night, but that day it was hanging down her back, very long and shiny. She asked me in and said, "Let me check my cookies."

I followed her and the aroma to the kitchen. She gave me a small container of chocolate-chip cookies to take home. Then she placed the heating pad in a bag and handed it to me. I thanked her and left.

When I got to the car, I said to Billy Joe, "I believe Eve is a natural beauty. Is she a model?"

He replied, "No, Baby, she's not."

I said, "Well, what does she do?"

He said, "She's a prostitute."

I was shocked. My mouth flew open. I said, "But she can't be; she was baking cookies."

Billy Joe laughed out loud and said, "Baby, prostitutes bake cookies, too."

Before we got to my place, Billy Joe said he wasn't hungry, so he would stop at the Varsity and get me something to go. He got curb service, and we carried the food home. As soon as we walked in the door, he threw the heating pad on the sofa and plugged it in.

Sitting there with the heating pad on his back, he told me he would be going out of town later that night with Harry and Tony. Then he said that they could pick him up there if I would take his car in for service the next morning. He had scheduled an appointment with Jim, the service writer at the Cadillac dealership, before he planned to be out of town. He really needed to get the new car serviced.

Billy Joe had been driving a midnight blue Cadillac the night I met him. He had recently purchased the new bronze Coupe de Ville. I couldn't understand why. He had said he wanted to keep a low profile. I wondered how in the world he could do that, driving around in a bronze car!

I told him I would take the car, but that I had to have cab fare to my office. He said, "Cab fare? What's wrong with the bus? It's on the bus line."

"There's nothing wrong with taking a cab," I said. "I'm not a 'babe in the woods' anymore."

He asked, "What's a cab got to do with a 'babe in the woods?'"

I told him how Harry acted, calling me a "babe in the woods," and rolling his eyes. I said, "I know I'm not because I asked Phoebe, and she told me it was someone who had not been around. Well, I can tell you I have been around. You should know. You were with me. I've been to Alabama, Mississippi, Louisiana, Texas, Oklahoma, Arkansas, North

Carolina, South Carolina, and Tennessee. So you can tell Harry I'm not a 'babe in the woods' anymore."

Billy Joe gave me a serious look and said, "I know you're not, Baby." I turned on my heel and went to the kitchen to get a Coke.

I could hear a noise in the living room, so I peeped around to see what it was. Billy Joe was lying on the sofa on his back with his arm covering his face, and he was shaking. I thought he was crying. I walked over to the sofa and asked, "What's wrong?" He didn't answer; he just kept shaking.

I tried to move his arm, but he wouldn't let me move it. Finally, I realized he was laughing. I started shaking his arm. "Don't laugh at me," I said.

With his arm still covering his face, he replied, "I'm not laughing at you, Baby. I'm laughing because I know why Harry thinks you're a 'babe in the woods.'"

"Then tell me," I cried.

"It's because you haven't been to Vegas! And that's where we're going soon."

So that explained it. Harry thought that if you had not been to Vegas, you were a "babe in the woods." Boy, was I relieved.

When Billy Joe left that night to meet Harry and Tony downstairs, he handed me a $20 bill. "Here's cab fare. Ten of it is a tip—for you, not the driver. But you knew that, didn't you? You're not a 'babe in the woods' anymore." I could hear him laughing as he walked down the hall to the elevator.

I went to the kitchen and threw the cookies in the garbage. I just couldn't eat those cookies.

The next morning, I was up before my wake-up service called. The wake-up service was a little extravagance I afforded after Al starting paying me to type his invoices on my lunch hour. I skipped coffee, rushed to get dressed, and took the car to Jim at the Cadillac dealership.

Jim removed some papers from the glove compartment and said, "Miss Augusta Billingsley. Follow me, please, Miss Billingsley." That's when I realized the car was in Aunt Aggie's name. I didn't know why the car was in her name. I knew his Aunt Aggie would never want to drive a car that big. How would she ever get it parked?

While Jim was checking in the car, one of the other guys asked if anyone else was going downtown. Jim told me they had a car headed downtown if I needed a ride. I told him I did. He handed me a copy of his write-up slip and pointed me in the direction of two other people who had the same destination.

On the way to work, I thought about the entire $20 I had saved Billy Joe. But then, I thought, "That's just my good luck. I'm not a 'babe in the woods' anymore."

A few nights later, when Billy Joe and I returned from dinner, there was a note in my door from a neighbor inviting me to a little get-together the next evening. I read aloud to Billy Joe. "We thought you would like to meet a few of your neighbors. If you don't have plans, drop in around seven o'clock."

I told Billy Joe I had met several neighbors at the elevators. Billy Joe said, "You're not in Overton now, Baby. You can't trust everybody you meet here. Sometimes you can be too friendly with folks. Don't you know that you're in the big city where some people will take advantage of the young and innocent waiting at elevators?"

His words sounded like a reprimand to me, so I said, "I don't plan to go to their get-together, but I'm twenty-four years old, Billy Joe, and I'm not young and innocent."

I thought about what one of Calhoun Johnson's clients had said one day in the office, and I had found the ideal time to use those words, so I added, "For your information, I've been around the block a few times myself."

Billy Joe looked as if he wanted to laugh. He was trying to wipe the smile off his face, but I could see the glimmer in his eye. His expression upset me, so I lashed out, "Well, I have."

He reached over, hugged me and said, "If you say so, Baby."

7.

The Magic Mirror

Billy Joe was on the phone, telling me that he was taking Tammy to the beauty shop for a hair trim. He said, "If we could have the pleasure of your company, Baby, we would go shopping afterwards."

I told him I would go. I was anxious to go; I wanted to see his daughter again. The first time I met Tammy, Billy Joe asked me to have pizza with them. He took us to Shakey's on Cheshire Bridge Road. The next time I saw Tammy, we went shopping and then stopped for pizza. Tammy liked pizza.

They picked me up an hour later, and we were on our way. When we arrived at The Magic Mirror, I observed that Billy Joe and Tammy knew everyone in the shop. Billy Joe's friend, Pete, was the owner of the Magic Mirror. Pete's wife, Susan, was a hairdresser.

The only person I knew was Emma, one of the hairdressers. I had met her shortly after I moved to Atlanta, when I lived with Lucky and Gina, his wife at that time. Emma had been working at a shop near Lucky's house, and she did my hair every week.

Emma told Billy Joe about the time I bleached my hair and it turned orange. She said, "It was 10:00 on a Sunday night. My doorbell was ringing, and I couldn't imagine who would be there so late. When I opened the door, there stood Jane with hair the color of carrots. I called her 'carrot-top' for a long time. I told her she would just have to go to work with orange hair on Monday. I didn't have a thing at home to re-do it."

After Tammy's haircut, we drove to Rich's downtown and ate in the Magnolia Room. Then we went to the shoe department and Tammy found exactly what she was looking for in a pair of shoes. Billy Joe winked at me as he paid for them.

As we walked through the store on the way out, I noticed how Tammy held her dad's hand. She would glance up at him in wonderment, as if she thought he was the tallest, best-looking and most remarkable person on earth. I thought so, too.

Cheryl, Billy Joe's ex-wife, was working in the yard when we took Tammy home. She walked over to the car, and Billy Joe introduced us. That was the first time I had met Cheryl. Billy Joe usually had Tammy with him when they picked me up on Saturdays, and they would drop me off first. Cheryl invited us in.

While Billy Joe and Tammy were in the kitchen getting out Cokes, Cheryl said to me, "I can see that he really cares about you, and you're having fun. He's a lot of fun if you're not married to him."

Billy Joe and Tammy brought the Cokes to the living room, and we all sat and chatted for several minutes. As we finished our Cokes and were leaving, Tammy was begging us to stay longer.

Billy Joe had arranged for us to meet Pete and Susan for dinner at the Diplomat that night. Since I had moved downtown, Billy Joe and I ate at the Diplomat frequently on weeknights.

I enjoyed being in Susan's company. She was a petite blonde. Pete was no more than 5'8" tall, of medium build, and wore his hair like a well-groomed hippie.

After dinner, we went to a couple of nightclubs. At the second one, we parked on a narrow street in front of the club. I usually had two drinks when we went out, and tonight was no different. We had wine with dinner and a drink at the dance club after dinner.

This club was just a dark lounge. There was a striking brunette at the microphone, singing *Cabaret*. Billy Joe ordered drinks for the third time that night. But I knew what he would do when they were served. Sure enough, he placed the palm of his hand over my glass while he was looking across the table and talking with Pete. Then he turned slowly and smiled at me. His gesture meant that I had consumed my apportionment.

One time Billy Joe had said, "There's nothing worse than having a drunk woman on your hands." He thought two drinks were enough for me.

Billy Joe usually had only one drink. He said he couldn't drink and be alert, and he needed to be alert. He was always paying attention to detail and being alert.

Other people arrived, laughing and talking. They spotted Billy Joe and Pete, and had started moving tables together when Billy Joe said it was about time for us to leave. We said our good-byes and went to the car.

Billy Joe asked me to drive as he ushered me around to the driver's side. After he got in, I started the car, pulled away from the curb and gently scraped Billy Joe's Cadillac against the side of Pete's new El Dorado. I stopped the car. Billy Joe turned toward me and looked me in the eye. He didn't say a word. Then, looking at him, I slowly eased the car forward, very carefully, scraping the cars together.

Billy Joe was still looking at me, mouth agape. I eased forward a little more until I had slowly scraped the cars together the length of both cars. I was looking at Billy Joe; he was looking at me—the whole time this slow scraping was happening. Then I stopped.

He said in a low, gentle, patient voice, "Baby, why did you do that?" I didn't have an answer. We sat there for a minute, looking into each other's eyes.

Then Billy Joe said, "Stay here while I go tell Pete." He went back inside the club. When he and Pete came out the door, he told me to drive away carefully so they could look at the damage. I couldn't understand what they were saying, but I did hear them chuckling.

Billy Joe got in the car. As I drove off, he said, "I told Pete that we won't bother with insurance—for him to just have it fixed and send me the bill." Then he changed the subject and never mentioned it again.

Two weeks later, we met Big Red for ribs at the Hickory House. Big Red had a tremendous appetite and his diet consisted of steak at Johnny Reb's, chicken at Kentucky Fried, and ribs at the Hickory House. Billy Joe had left the table to speak with some people he knew who were waiting at the door. That's when Big Red told me that he followed Billy Joe to the body shop to have the car repaired. Pete met them there. When Pete drove up, Big Red said, "Here comes Pete with the Magic Mirror."

The owner of the body shop had already examined the damage to Billy Joe's car. When he saw the identical marks on Pete's El Dorado, he said, "I see what you mean. These scrape marks are a mirror image. It does look a little like magic to me."

Big Red's rotund body was shaking with laughter as he said, "He had no idea that Magic Mirror was the name of Pete's beauty shop. I'll get a lot of miles out of that one. Since you've come into Billy Joe's life, I've been able to add a lot of unique and amusing stories to my repertoire. Without a doubt, this one is beyond compare."

We saw Pete and Susan several times after that, but they didn't mention the cars. I was sorry about both cars, but I didn't worry about it. I remembered that I had heard Lucky say, "People who have money don't have problems; they have another expense." Billy Joe just had another expense.

Billy Joe left the next day to go out of town, and Phoebe and I met at Lenox. We browsed through Rich's and a couple of the smaller shops. While we were having lunch, I told her about scraping the two cars together. She said, "I know how men are about cars. He's too good to be true. And he didn't say another thing about it?"

I told her the next thing he mentioned was that he would have to leave the next day. She asked me what I thought about Billy Joe staying gone so much.

"Phoebe, I'm glad he's gone so much of the time. I can't stand to be smothered. My Aunt Maggie told me that when I was a little girl, I would go around singing *Don't Fence Me In*. She said I had been independent since I was a small child."

I continued, "Usually, when you see the same man all the time, you have to answer to him. It's almost like being married. He wants to know what time you'll be home and what you're going to eat. It's different with Billy Joe. He never asks what time I'll be home and he never asks what we're going to eat. He suggests things, and I say, 'That sounds good to me.'"

Phoebe asked, "Don't you ever cook?"

I just laughed. "Phoebe, you know I don't have time to cook. Billy Joe called one time and said, 'I think I'll cook a steak.' He brought two filet mignons, potatoes, lettuce and tomatoes. He took out my big iron skillet and placed it on the gas flame until it was real hot. Then he threw the steak in. His steaks almost burned on the outside, but he called it 'sealing in the flavor.' I boiled the potatoes, put butter on them, and stuck them under the broiler to brown. Then I made the salad, and we were ready to eat."

I mentioned the spaghetti I cooked for him one time. I had made a big pot of spaghetti sauce and let it simmer two hours. Billy Joe called and asked if I would like to go eat. I told him I had made spaghetti sauce and suggested he pick up some lettuce and tomatoes, and we could just eat at my place.

"Phoebe, you won't believe what a production he made of using the fork and spoon rolling that spaghetti. I had always cut my spaghetti with a fork. Half the sauce was left in my plate that night. It came off the spaghetti when I rolled it in the spoon."

I told her that when we finished eating, Billy Joe looked across the table at me and said, "That was real good, Baby. I didn't know you could cook."

"I could cook more than I do, but we don't just sit around in the apartment. We go places and do things. When I was a teenager, Daddy called that going out to 'see and be seen.' It's more fun with Billy Joe than it was then."

Phoebe said, "Well, if he doesn't get mad about your scraping his new car, what does he get mad about? Is there anything that irritates him?"

I admitted, "The way I rattle on sometimes probably irritates him, but he never shows it. By the time my talking gets on his nerves, he has to go out of town. We've never had an argument, and we're always happy to see each other. So now do you know why I don't mind if he's gone? I love things the way they are."

After lunch, we shopped a while longer. The stores were closing at six o'clock, but we went inside Mori Luggage & Gifts before we left. At that time, it was downstairs facing the parking lot, near the cafeteria. Billy Joe was intrigued by everything in that shop. There was much more than luggage to see. I looked at the executive gifts, and thought I would buy Mr. Green's Christmas present there in a few months. It was too early to choose a Christmas present when the temperature was still over ninety degrees outside.

We walked on to our cars in the parking lot. Phoebe suggested I drop by her apartment and see her new placemats. I did, knowing I would be home by eleven o'clock. Billy Joe usually called at eleven. If I wasn't home by then, he didn't call again until the next night. And he never asked where I had been.

I had learned a lot about being courteous from Billy Joe. I showed him the same courtesy. I never asked where he had been either. When he had to go out of town, I never asked when he would return. I didn't even ask where he was going. Sometimes he told me where he would be; other times, he didn't.

He had given me the unlisted phone numbers of Mark in Biloxi, and Ruth at Burl's Motel. He gave me Victor's number in Birmingham, but I had never met Victor. I had several other numbers to call "in case of emergency." I didn't ask what he called an "emergency," but I thought I would know when to call the numbers.

One time Billy Joe said, "At least I can give you credit for having good sense." I don't remember what prompted him to say that, but I did know that I had always had it. I classified "good sense" as "common sense." People had told me that I had common sense. That's because I was from Overton. Everyone in Overton had common sense. We were born with it. Those who weren't born with it learned it by association. I had no desire to live there, but I was proud to be from Overton.

8.

Family Reunion

Billy Joe phoned early one Sunday morning. He said, "Dress like you're going to church, Baby. I've got a surprise for you." And boy, was it a surprise! He didn't wear a suit, so I could see that we were not going to church. He wore a white polo-type sweater and black slacks.

I said, "Obviously, we are not going to church, so tell me where we're going." He just beamed and said, "If I told you, then it wouldn't be a surprise."

He drove for about 30 minutes, and finally he said, "I hope you don't mind, but I have not been to my family reunion in years, so I thought today would be a good day to go. In fact, it's been so long, you'll probably know more people there than I will. Aunt Aggie is so happy we're going that she said, 'I always take plenty of food for everybody. Ya'll don't have to take a thing.'"

He turned down a tree-lined street with large white houses. There was one house with green shutters, a green roof, and a country-style front porch complete with rocking chairs. A multitude of cars had been parked in the street, on the lawn, and all around the house. He drove up the driveway and around to the back yard.

When he stopped the car, he turned and looked at me. I could see the uncertainty in his face. It was that same look of uncertainty he had on his face the night of our first date, when I opened the door. I wanted to say something or do something to make him feel at ease.

But then he got out, came around, opened my door, and we slowly headed for the people in the back yard. I heard somebody say, "It's Billy

Joe." Then several people came toward us. Two of the men were shaking his hand; women were hugging him, and the children were running around us screaming and playing.

I thought to myself, "This is almost like church; they're treating him as if he's a prodigal son."

Billy Joe was right. I did know quite a few in his family. They all came up and hugged me, and he introduced me to some people I didn't know. Others came up, hugged me and introduced themselves. I had never seen Billy Joe look so happy.

One of his younger cousins gazed at my diamond ring. She said, "It must be nice to have a boyfriend who will buy you a diamond ring like that." I didn't have the heart to tell her that I had purchased it myself and it took me two years to pay for it.

Aunt Aggie had ridden up with Billy Joe's sister, Liz, and her five children. Liz was married to a successful businessman. Of course he was successful. His job was a sure thing, being married to Liz. He worked in the Billingsley family business, and the only thing he had to do was show up every day. The children kept Liz busy. Billy Joe and I had been to her house once. The son was shy, but he was cute. And the four little girls were beautiful, just like Liz.

I saw a gallon of red Kool-Aid on the kitchen counter, and I knew Aunt Aggie had brought it. I asked Billy Joe if he drank a lot of Kool-Aid at home when he was growing up. He replied, "No more than anybody else. Why do you ask?"

I told him that his Aunt Aggie made Kool-Aid and cookies for us when we attended Vacation Bible School, and we wondered if he had it every day. Hers was better than the Kool-Aid that anybody else made.

He said, "That's because she added pineapple juice, or some kind of juice. That's what made it taste different. It had more body to it. And you're right, she does make good Kool-Aid. I'd never thought about it before. How do you think of all these things?"

Cheryl and Tammy came in the door. Tammy ran to her dad, and Billy Joe picked her up, swung her around, and then sat down with Tammy in his lap. She had Billy Joe's eyes, and I could tell she would grow up to be tall. It was no surprise to see Cheryl at the reunion. She and Billy Joe had been divorced several years, but Billy Joe had said, "It's not her fault; she was a good wife. All of it was my fault. I couldn't stay home, and she couldn't live with that." And he adored Tammy.

On the way home, Billy Joe told me about his four cousins who lived on a hill next to a construction site on the main highway when they were boys. His cousins would go down and play on the equipment some days after the workers had gone for the day. As luck would have it, one of them managed to get the bulldozer started, and he did a lot of damage before he figured out how to stop it. The sheriff's department was called, and the boys were knee-deep in trouble. Their dad had to pay for the damage, and the boys were not allowed to go near the machinery again.

Billy Joe said that one day the boys were walking to school and the construction crew was starting their day. The bulldozer operator was having a difficult time getting the bulldozer started that morning. His little cousin hollered out, "You want me to crank that thing for you?" He said that the operator got off and chased the boys halfway to school.

Billy Joe said, "I really enjoyed today. I wish I could feel part of a family all the time. I also wish I still had my old friends from high school. They were real friends. We could always get in touch with each other—unlike the friends I have now. We did some gruesome stuff in school, or what people called gruesome stuff back then, but it was all in fun.

"I remember one time I had been away a year or two, and I went down to play cards with a few of them. They were playing for high stakes. I didn't want to bet that much—I just wanted to win enough to get my clothes out of the cleaners."

He was still talking about Harley, Little Bee, and all his old buddies when we got back to my place. He sat down on the sofa, staring out the sliding glass door, and said, "Baby, it really ruins a person's life when they have to go to prison at such a young age. I felt so alone." He told me how the other inmates raped the new prisoners, and how the guards beat them. He said that he thought his father's beatings were bad, but those were mild compared to what the guards did to him.

"The thing that hurt the most was seeing the look on Aunt Aggie's face just before I had to go serve my time. I said to her, 'Aggie'—I called her Aggie when I wanted something—'Aggie, I want you to stop walking around here crying and wringing your hands'—She would wring her hands when she was worried—'That's not gonna help a thing. I'll be back and then we can start over.'

"Harley drove me to the bus station. If I had known then what I know now, I would have taken a bus headed in the opposite direction from Kansas. But, no, I had to go take my punishment as a man. I thought it would make me a better person. Instead, it left me with a dislike for people in authority, and I've tried to defy anyone in authority since then. I can't help it, Baby."

He sat in silence while tears ran down his face. I went over and sat next to him. He took my hand, and we sat quietly for a long, long time.

I thought of all the animosity between Billy Joe and his father. I had asked him one time why he didn't work in his father's business. He told me that he had tried it three times, and it didn't work out for either of them. Now I understood more about why Billy Joe didn't have a real job.

I knew other people who didn't have a real job. Fred Powell from Overton had worked for a jewelry store, and one day he decided he didn't want a real job either. So he sold jewelry out of the trunk of his car. He also sold small appliances and other odds and ends.

Billy Joe sold merchandise, including jewelry, out of his trunk. Fred sold to retail customers; Billy Joe's customers bought wholesale. Fred and Billy Joe were both self-employed. I knew that Fred made a good living just "wheeling and dealing." So did Billy Joe.

9.

Biloxi

My day at work had been horrific! A meeting for 200 people was to be held at the Marriott in two weeks, and I was responsible for all the arrangements. Usually it was easy working for Mr. Green, and he didn't expect a lot from me. I remembered one day before I moved downtown to be near the office, Mr. Green had said to me, "Jane, I don't ask a lot from you, but I do expect you to be here promptly at nine o'clock."

He didn't know how difficult that was at times.

For instance, there was the weekend Billy Joe had to go to Biloxi and asked me to ride down with him. He planned to have me back on Sunday night. We arrived in Biloxi late Saturday afternoon. After we checked into the Broadwater Beach, Billy Joe said, "Why don't we go to the pool? I know you brought your bathing suit."

I had brought my Cole of California bikini. It was a conservative hip-hugger, and the top had underwire and fiber-filled cups. I loved classy, expensive bathing suits and had purchased my first grownup bathing suit when I was only seventeen.

I would always remember March of 1960. I was attending a party on a Saturday night at the home of Claire who lived in a small community just south of Overton. Claire had invited three of us to spend the night. She was an only child whose parents would allow her to have as many guests as the house would accommodate so long as there were beds for everyone and we didn't have to sleep on pallets on the floor.

Claire's grandmother and aunt lived next door. I called her "Aunt Estelle," although she was not my real aunt. She was at least fifty years old and had gray hair. Aunt Estelle had never married, and in those days, some people referred to her as an "old maid." I was amused at the expression on her face every time she looked surprised at something we had done. Her eyes would turn big and round—you could see them through her glasses—and her eyebrows would shoot straight up. Then she would hold her hands up to her mouth, with bracelets jingling, and say, "My word!"

The weather was unusually cold for March, and on that Saturday night there was the biggest ice storm most people could remember. The phones were out, and the roads were closed. By Tuesday, although we could not get to Overton because of trees and power lines being down, we did manage to hitch a ride to Griffin with Aunt Estelle as she drove to work at Clayton Furniture.

The roads were treacherous, but we made it to Griffin. She parked the car in the parking lot behind Clayton Furniture and said, "You girls can go shopping, but be back here at twelve o'clock. I'm taking you to Abigail's Tea Room for lunch."

The four of us got out of the car and carefully walked up the icy sidewalk on the main street toward the clothing stores and McClellan's, a five-and-dime. We browsed through several of the stores, and then we stopped at McClellan's and sat in a booth drinking Cokes and talking for a long time.

On the way back down the street, we saw bathing suits on display in the window of an exclusive dress shop called Goldstein's. I said, "I have an idea. Why don't we all buy a bathing suit?"

Claire replied, "With ice on the ground? Are you crazy, or what?"

"Or what!" I replied, as I opened the door to the store. I immediately saw the one I wanted. It was a one-piece suit in light brown patterned with green leaves, a Rose Marie Reid. I tried it on. "Perfect fit," my friends said.

I dressed, picked up the bathing suit and carried it to the cash register. The price was $17.98, which was an astronomical price for a bathing suit at that time, since we could buy a nice blouse for less than $5.00.

The lady asked if I would like to charge it. I answered, "Yes ma'am."

She called her office to get approval. Then she turned to me and asked, "Miss Moss, do you have an account with us?"

"No ma'am."

"Would you like to open one?"

"Yes ma'am."

She asked, "Could you give me a reference, please?"

I answered, "Yes ma'am. Aunt Estelle Caldwell. She works at Clayton Furniture."

The lady picked up the phone and called Clayton Furniture. She asked for Aunt Estelle. After explaining to Aunt Estelle that Jane Moss would like to make a charge in the amount of $17.98 and asking if that met with her approval, the lady replaced the receiver and handed me a sales slip for my signature. It was that simple. Thanks to Aunt Estelle, I had opened an account at Goldstein's at the age of seventeen.

We left the store and giggled hysterically as we walked through the ice on the way back to Clayton Furniture. We had to wait a few minutes for Aunt Estelle to finish her work so we could go to lunch. Finally she came out of the office carrying her big brown handbag, and we headed for the car in the back parking lot.

After we were seated in Abigail's, Aunt Estelle asked if we had purchased anything interesting during our all-morning-shopping spree. We all said in unison, "A bathing suit."

Aunt Estelle exclaimed, "My word!" Her hands went to her mouth and the bracelets jingled. We tried to stifle our giggles; after all, we were in Abigail's Tea Room.

I told Billy Joe about the Rose Marie Reid bathing suit as we walked to the pool. He was still laughing about it as we entered the pool area.

We had to walk halfway around the pool to the unoccupied lounge chairs. I saw several couples and a small group of beautiful blondes sitting around talking and laughing. They looked up and smiled as we passed. I hated parading in front of all those gorgeous people. Weighing only 104 pounds, even my underwired, fiber-filled cups created little or no cleavage. Going to the pool was not a number one priority because Billy Joe and I spent most of the weekend in his car, so my minimal suntan was quite a contrast to Billy Joe's bronze skin. I was feeling very self-conscious walking past those suntanned people. In fact, I felt as if I had four feet, and I just knew I would stumble over one of them.

Billy Joe reached over, took my hand, and led me to two lounge chairs. He could always sense when I felt uncomfortable, and that's when he would make physical contact by taking my hand or reaching around my shoulder and hugging me. He was always attentive to me.

Billy Joe and I had been at the pool for less than an hour, sitting in the lounge chairs, talking and luxuriating in the sun. The weather was too hot and humid to stay longer unless I planned to get in the water to cool off. I had no intention of getting my hair wet and having to start over with a shampoo. Hair dryers at that time had only 210 watts.

Billy Joe sensed that I was ready to go back to the room. He stood up, picked up his towel and threw it over his shoulder. When he looked down at me and smiled, I realized he was thinking of how long it would take me to get dressed if I had to shampoo my hair. He was usually considerate of my hair.

After we showered and dressed, Billy Joe made a phone call and I heard him say, "We'll be right over."

We drove east on Highway 90 and turned left on a narrow road. It was almost dark and I couldn't see well, but I could tell there were several houses, and they seemed to be in a circle. On the left was the home of his friends, Mark and Colleen.

I had met Mark on a previous trip, but I had not met his wife. The first time I saw Mark, I was surprised that he reminded me of Al at the print shop. He looked to be in his late thirties and was a little less than six feet tall. His glasses had thick lenses that were almost identical to Al's.

Mark came to the door and led us into a large country kitchen where Colleen was cooking dinner. She asked me to have a seat in one of the chairs around the table. Billy Joe and Mark sat in the den and talked.

The children were in and out of the kitchen while Colleen finished dinner. After about twenty minutes, Colleen called everybody in to eat. She served red beans and rice.

I said, "This is a real 'tasty' dish, Colleen. 'Tasty' is Billy Joe's favorite word when it comes to food." Billy Joe smiled at me.

Mark spoke up and said, "Looks like you've done well recently, Billy Joe. I'm glad to see it. It's about time you were dealt some good cards."

After dinner, Mark said to Billy Joe, "Have you been to see Mama yet?"

Billy Joe said, "No, I thought we'd see her in the morning."

Mark replied, "Good. Let's ride down to the bingo hall." Billy Joe asked me to stay with Colleen and the children. He said he would be back later. I wanted to play bingo, but since he didn't ask me to go, I stayed.

Colleen was a pretty brunette. She wore little makeup, and she acted relaxed. The children were well behaved. Trena, the daughter, showed me her dolls and all the other things she could drag from her room. We had fun playing.

Mark and Billy Joe returned at midnight. Billy Joe said that he thought we would get on back to the hotel since he had a lot to do the next day. We said our good-byes and left.

On the way back to the Broadwater, I said, "Billy Joe, you have such nice friends. How do you meet all these nice people?"

He looked over at me, smiled, and said, "I get around, Baby."

The next morning after brunch, Billy Joe and I drove up to Burl's Motel. It was a small, older place and was run by Ruth, a lady in her mid-fifties. She was happy to see Billy Joe, and that made her happy to see me, too. I observed the manner in which Ruth answered her phone. It was obvious that she was a shrewd businesswoman.

We sat and chatted for about thirty minutes, then Billy Joe told her he had some things to take care of while he was there, so we had better be going. On the way back to the Broadwater, I asked Billy Joe if Ruth was Mark's Mother. He said, "No, she's just been a good friend for a long time."

I told Billy Joe that I had listened to the way she talked on the phone and that I wanted to be like her one day. He said, "No you don't, Baby. You don't want to be like anyone else. Just be yourself."

Billy Joe dropped me off at the Broadwater and said, "I'll be back in an hour or so. Why don't you go to the pool?" I told him I would rather stay in the cool room and read. I had no intention of parading around those tanned sun worshipers—not with my pale skin.

At three o'clock, Billy Joe called and told me he would be a little while longer. I said, "That's okay, as long as I get to work by nine o'clock in the morning."

"Don't worry. I promise you'll be there," he said. I wasn't worried. It was only a six-hour drive.

I thought how different this trip was from my last trip to Biloxi. I had flown down on a Saturday afternoon for dinner. Billy Joe and I left early Sunday morning for the drive back home. I wasn't stuck in the hotel room that time. On Saturday night, we had dinner with an attorney and a group of Billy Joe's friends who were local businessmen, and some of the wives or girlfriends. The dinner was at a nice restaurant, and all the men wore suits. Billy Joe had worn one of his silk suits that night. I was thinking how strange it had been seeing Billy Joe in a silk suit again. He had stopped wearing silk suits after I told him what one of the artists in Mr. Phillips' office had said.

The artist came in the office one morning and told us that he had dinner at the new Regency the night before. He said he saw pimps wearing silk suits, with their prostitutes on their arms, down at the Regency. I told Billy Joe that I hoped none of the people in my office had seen us the night we were with Harry, Renee, Tony and Eve. After that, Billy Joe wore business suits when we went out in Atlanta—almost identical to those worn by Mr. Phillips and Mr. Green. If it's true that "clothes make the man," then Billy Joe was a real businessman in those suits! And Billy Joe never took me back to the Regency.

I didn't have to wait for him on that last trip. It's not that waiting was difficult for me. I had spent hours on end waiting for Billy Joe, in one place or another, and I had spent most of that time reading.

Reading was a favorite pastime, and I had plenty of time to catch up during this trip. It was seven o'clock when Billy Joe called again and said, "I'll be there in a few minutes; be ready to go." When he arrived, he was in a big hurry. He rushed me to the car with my one heavily loaded tote bag. Fortunately I had brought plenty to keep me busy in the room.

There was a man sitting in the back seat of the car. As he opened my door, Billy Joe said, "Baby, this is Jamie. He's gonna ride with us." Then he went around and got in the driver's seat.

After he headed out in the traffic, he said, "We need to hurry to get you to the airport in Gulfport for the last flight to Atlanta. You can take a cab home. I'm sorry, Baby, but I can't leave here tonight."

I replied, "Okay, I thought Jamie was hitching a ride to Atlanta."

Jamie laughed and said, "Billy Joe told me you were easy to get along with, Jane. He said the only problem he had was having to rush to an airport to get you back to work on time. You're a rare employee."

At that point, I wanted to ask Jamie where he worked, but Billy Joe had told me a long time ago not to ask his friends where they worked. "It makes them feel uncomfortable around you, Baby," he had said.

They talked about the clubs Mark owned. I had seen some of those clubs and, without going inside, I could tell they were strip joints. Billy Joe had told me that some of his friends owned those clubs, and the area was called "The Strip." I didn't realize Mark would be one of the owners. Jamie was saying something else that I didn't quite hear when Billy Joe said, "Watch it!" I figured Jamie was saying something Billy Joe didn't want me to hear. He was always saying, "Watch it!" to Harry. Then there was silence.

So, to make conversation, I said to Jamie, "I hope we get there on time. Billy Joe drives so slowly. He usually asks me to drive in the daytime, but I have to drive the speed limit, come to a complete stop, don't weave, and don't do anything to get stopped. I don't even do the California Roll anymore."

Jamie asked, "What's the California Roll?"

I said, "Billy Joe, I thought you had told everyone you knew about the California Roll."

Billy Joe replied, "Well, I guess I missed telling Jamie." Then he proceeded to tell him.

"I went to school with this ol' boy named Harley Gibson. We were best friends. Harley went in the service after he graduated, and when he was discharged, he took a job in Atlanta. He didn't like having to drive up there every day, so he became a policeman. Meanwhile, he got married and had a bunch of little boys that are going to be as tall and lanky as he is."

Billy Joe turned and looked at me, then he continued, "He was telling me that one of the most prominent women in Overton came in the police station to argue her case about a ticket that she had been given for running a stop sign. Harley told her that what she did was apply the brakes, and then roll on through the stop sign. Harley said to her, in his best Southern accent, 'That's what is known as the California Roll, Mrs. Jackson, and in Georgia, that's against the law. In Georgia, we call it running a stop sign.'

"Harley said she was real mad, but she paid the fine. Then the next time he ran into her in the grocery store, she turned her nose in the air and went the other way."

We all laughed. I had heard that story so many times from Billy Joe. But every time he imitated Harley's Southern drawl, I just cracked up again.

I said, "Billy Joe, tell us some more about you and Harley."

Billy Joe said, "I had a Chrysler New Yorker one time. I remember taking Harley with me up to Braxton Creek to pick up a load of moonshine. I didn't tell him where I was headed when I called him. I just told him I wanted him to ride somewhere with me. He met me at the gas station on Central Avenue in Hapeville and left his car parked there.

"We talked and laughed all the way up to Braxton Creek. I stopped at a diner on the main highway and told Harley I had to go somewhere and I'd be back in a few minutes. He had no idea where I was going. I left him at the diner while I went on to pick up the moonshine.

"When I returned to the diner, he opened the car door and looked in the back seat where I had moonshine loaded from bottom to top.

"He asked, 'What's all that?' He looked at me for a minute and then said, 'I don't think I'd better ride back with you.' But he got in the car anyway. Both of us knew there was no cab in Braxton Creek. I drove off, and by the time I went through the only traffic light in Braxton Creek, I was hitting 120 miles an hour. I thought Harley was gonna jump out."

"I can't believe you ever drove that fast, Billy Joe."

He said, "You didn't know me back then."

"What else did Harley say?" I wanted to hear Billy Joe imitate Harley's Southern drawl again.

"Baby, I don't think he said another word all the way back to his car. I had to do all the talking. After that, he was hesitant getting in the car with me. I didn't do anything else like that with Harley in the car. We'd been friends too long."

I said, "I don't think my Mustang will go 120 miles an hour."

Jamie said, "A Mustang is a nice little car for her, Billy Joe. Did you buy it new?"

Billy Joe replied, "No, she already had it. I think she paid it off with money her uncle gave her. He calls it her retirement fund, but Jane has started calling it her trust fund. That's because one of the girls in her office building asked her where she lived. When Jane told her, the girl said she thought only prostitutes and rich people lived in that building, and did she have a trust fund, or what?

"Jane felt insulted, but she thinks fast. She told the girl she had a trust fund, and that her uncle set it up. Since that day, Jane has been calling it her trust fund. She's probably got $200 in it."

Jamie laughed so hard, I thought he would get the hiccups.

I noticed the way Billy Joe referred to me as Jane. He called me "Baby", but when he referred to me, he said "Jane." Most of my friends called me "Janie," but Billy Joe never used that name.

The three of us got out at the airport. Billy Joe purchased my ticket, checked my bag, and gave me cab fare. He hugged me and said, "I'll call you, Baby."

As they walked away, I heard Jamie say, "Billy Joe, you are one lucky son-of-a-gun."

I was thinking how lucky I was to be able to get to work on time.

10.

Grits, Eggs, and Chicken Pot Pie

Billy Joe called one night to see if I wanted to go to Eng's downtown for stir-fried shrimp. Oriental food was not his favorite, but he seemed to enjoy watching the food being cooked before his eyes at Eng's. He said he had tried to call several times earlier and thought I was probably out shopping with Phoebe, but he was glad he had tried one more time.

I told him I couldn't go because I was making a dress and had to finish it by morning. I planned to drop it off downstairs at the cleaners to have it steam pressed. He said, "Well, what will you eat?" I told him I had no idea, but I was sure I had some grits, eggs and frozen chicken pot pie there, so I didn't think I would starve.

"Having it there and eating it are two different things. You don't even think about eating when you're sewing," said Billy Joe. "We'll go to Eng's another time. Tonight, Harry and I will go eat, and then I'll bring you something real tasty. In that way, I'll know you ate."

I said, "Billy Joe, you're out of town most of the time. Do you think I starve when you're gone?"

He replied, "No, Baby, I don't think you starve, but I learned a long time ago that man cannot live by grits, eggs and chicken pot pie alone. He must have salad with steak, chicken or ribs. So, what do you want with your salad?"

"Steak, chicken and ribs all sound good to me," I said.

He replied, "It'll be a while." I kept sewing.

A few minutes before nine o'clock, the doorbell rang. I hopped up from the sewing machine and went to the door. There stood Billy Joe and Harry. I didn't know why he brought Harry. I didn't like Harry, and Billy Joe knew that. Harry's bright blue eyes had a brooding look, and if he ever looked at me, I felt his eyes piercing all the way through me. I had never heard him laugh out loud like Billy Joe. Harry would give a little laugh under his breath and turn his head at the same time, signifying that whatever you said was a little funny, but then you were dismissed.

Billy Joe took the "to-go" box to the kitchen. He opened it, and there was the biggest steak I had ever seen. I said, "Billy Joe, you know I never get a steak that big. That's enough for three meals for me."

He just laughed and said, "That's the point, Baby. I'll know you will have plenty for two more days, if you'll take the time to eat it." He took a plate and salad bowl out of the cabinet and started fixing a plate. I removed my sewing items from the dining room table. He brought the plate, a Coke on ice and a glass of water to the table. Billy Joe wanted me to drink water. He said it was good for me and would keep my skin glowing. And that it would also keep me from having kidney problems later on in life. The only times I drank water were when Billy Joe was around and when I was real thirsty.

Billy Joe glanced over at Harry and said, "It makes me feel more secure when she has something to eat. I remember one time when I was in high school, I ran away with Karen Keller. I didn't even date the girl. We were just hanging out together one day, and she said she was running away from home. So I went with her. Pretty soon we had no money and nowhere to go. Karen got hungry and wanted to go home, so I took her back home.

"Later she started seeing Winston McDonald, and they were planning to get married. I was riding around with Winston one day and I said, 'Winston, you know that when you marry a girl, you've got to feed her. You can't take her home when she gets hungry. Why don't we go rob a bank?' Winston looked at me as if he thought I was serious. I was just trying to give the boy some good advice."

I had finished eating, and Billy Joe was clearing off the table. Harry had walked over to the dress I was making. He asked me why I made my clothes. I told him there was one thing I could do, and that was save money. The best way to do that was not spend money on too many expensive clothes.

I told him that I could go down to Joseph's and put a dress on lay-a-way for $36.00. By the time I got it out of lay-a-way, I had already made and worn three other dresses for less than that. And they didn't look "home-made," either.

Billy Joe walked over and picked up the dress. It was an A-line mini dress. The material was an off-white background with large strokes of black curly cues. The neck was round and it had a four-inch placket about two inches wide with hidden buttons on the front. The sleeves were long and skinny. That was the style then.

I said, "Billy Joe, I made that one from a Vogue pattern. It has more style than the other patterns, don't you think?"

Harry spoke up and said, "Why are you always saying to Billy Joe, 'Don't you think?' He doesn't have to think when he's around you. Your brain must work overtime to come up with all the things you think. You think enough for both of you, with some left over."

Billy Joe ignored Harry and said, "I like this one, Baby." Then he looked on the table and saw a letter addressed to me from Carte Blanche.

"I didn't know you had a Carte Blanche credit card," he said.

"I don't." I replied. "I sent in an application, and that's a letter from them telling me that I can't have one because my income is too low."

Billy Joe said, "It shouldn't be, not with what you make plus the money Al pays you. You make as much as a cheap divorce lawyer."

I said, "I know I do, but you know how they discriminate against women. A few years ago, I worked with Tina Hudson. When she married Bobby Williams, she sent in a name change to the department stores. One of them sent her a new application to fill out. She filled in Bobby's name as her spouse. When the new credit cards came, they were in the name of Robert S. Williams. She called the credit department and told them that she wanted the card in her new name, Tina H. Williams. They told her it would have to be in her husband's name since she was married. Now do you call that fair? It was her card to begin with. But she couldn't get them to put it in her married name. So she's still using the card with Bobby's name on it."

Billy Joe asked, "How much did they say you had to make before you could qualify for a card?"

I replied, "They didn't say how much, but when I filled out the application, I didn't include the money Al pays me. Al said not to report the money—that we would use the barter system. I asked him what he meant, and he told me that the barter system was when you traded things. He said, 'I have money, and you have a talent to type my invoices, so it's just a trade-off. I won't be taking out taxes.'

"So I know I can't report it. That would get Al into trouble with the IRS. But not me, I didn't do anything."

That's when Harry spoke up again and said, "Yeah, boy. You're learning, kid."

I said, "Harry, you don't know how much I've learned about money. I had to read that letter twice. I was afraid Carte Blanche had learned that I zeroed out my checking account, even though that was over a year ago."

I told them about the day Mr. Patrick, a Vice President with the Trust Company, called me at work and asked why I had closed my checking account.

I said, "I haven't closed it."

Mr. Patrick told me he didn't think I had, so he would see what happened and get back to me. I knew Mr. Patrick would find out what happened. He was a friend of Paul Roberts, the lawyer at Atlanta Federal. And Paul worked with Lucky's wife, Gina. Paul was the one who had set up the appointment for an interview that landed my first job in Atlanta in 1961. It was a temporary job with a friend of his, another lawyer,

Calhoun Johnson. He also sent me to see Mr. Patrick at the Trust Company. He said Mr. Patrick would handle all my banking needs.

Thirty minutes later, my phone at work rang again. It was Mr. Patrick. He said, "Janie, you'll never believe it. You have just zeroed out your checking account by writing checks to equal the exact balance you had in the bank. The computer automatically zeros you out when that happens. I don't know anybody else who could do that, even if they tried. How did you do it?"

I told him I simply paid all my bills, and I had no way of knowing it would zero out. He thought it was funny. Then he told me that if I would bring all my bills in, we could sit down and work out a budget so that it wouldn't happen again.

The next week, I called Mr. Patrick and asked him if I could come over on my lunch hour and bring all my bills. He saw me as I walked through the front door, and motioned for me to come on into his office. I set the shoebox on his desk.

Mr. Patrick asked, "What's in that shoebox?" I told him it was full of bills. He started laughing, and then he sat down and opened the box.

He went through all the mail on top, shook his head and said, "You owe less than $300.00, but you use too many credit cards. Why don't you pay off all of them, and in the future, use only one card? In that way, you won't have to write so many checks. That should keep you from zeroing out your account again."

So that's what I did. He made a transfer from my savings account to my checking account so that I could pay the balance on my next statements. He told me I could start over. When I was leaving, he walked me to the front door and said, "By the way, I want you to know I like that shoebox."

When I finished telling the story, Billy Joe and Harry looked at each other. Harry said, "Vice presidents and lawyers, how about that!"

Then Billy Joe said, "Well, you need to use all those shoeboxes for something." They both looked amused. I was sorry I had told them about zeroing out my account.

"I think we'll let you get back to your sewing. Are you going bowling tomorrow night?" asked Billy Joe.

I replied, "I don't know yet. I will need to get a ride with someone in the office building, and after bowling, they will have to bring me home. Didn't I tell you that my car wouldn't start? It's down at Pam's house. Her husband, Marvin, is going to repair it.

"I stopped by their house last Sunday night, and when I was leaving, they walked out to the car with me. Marvin said, 'Why don't you get a good car the next time; that Ford Mustang won't do nothing.' I had started the car, and it was in Park, so I stepped on the accelerator and raced the motor. It made a loud noise. Then it went dead and wouldn't start again. He laughed at first, and then he saw I had a problem. He said he could fix it. So they brought me home and dropped me at the door. Marvin can fix a car as well as any mechanic at Bert's filling station."

Billy Joe knew Bert, so he understood what I was saying. Bert always had a mechanic on duty and people in Overton could trust him with their car. I told Billy Joe about the Saturday I was in Overton and the Mustang was making a funny noise. I turned into the independent gas station and drove within six feet of the front door, rolled down the window and said to Bert, "Come out here and listen to this."

There were several men sitting in the station. Slow walking, slow talking Bert ambled toward the door. He said, "What is it?"

"It won't do it now, but it was making a noise like "Grrrrr Ahhhh.""

The mechanic walked over and stood by Bert. He said, "I'm not sure. Do that again."

I went, "Grrrrr Ahhhh." They both laughed out loud.

Bert asked, "How often does it do it?"

"It's only done it twice this morning."

Bert shook his head and said, "It's still under warranty. Just take it to the dealer. We'd have to charge you to check it out and repair it. Do you think it'll make it to the dealer?"

"I don't know. That's why I came by here first. And now it won't do it."

He said, "Well, if it does it again in a few blocks, just bring it back and we'll take a look at it. If it stops on the way home, call us. I'll send the wrecker. Don't want you to be stranded."

"Thanks, Bert. See ya'll later," I said, as I drove off.

I told Billy Joe I made it home that day, and I didn't remember the Mustang ever making that noise again.

Billy Joe said, "Well, you know you can use my car, if you need one. There's a key in the second drawer in the kitchen. I've paid parking out there through this month."

"Billy Joe, you know I don't like to use your car. It's bad enough that you park it in my garage, and the neighbors think you live here. What would everybody think if I started driving around in a Cadillac?"

Harry gave that little laugh under his breath and turned his head again. Then he opened the door and stepped out into the hallway.

Billy Joe tilted my chin up with his finger, so that I would be looking him in the eye, and said, "I'm going out of town for a while. Don't sit here and sew. You know I want you to get out, go places, and do things, so that you'll be a well-rounded person. I'll call you, Baby." He hugged me and left.

11.

Lawyers and Politicians

Billy Joe phoned a few days later. When I told him I was sewing, he said, "Baby, you don't need to stay at home and sew. Remember what I told you. I want you to get out and do other things so you'll be a well-rounded person."

I replied, "Billy Joe, I don't have time to be any more well-rounded than I am now. I don't sit at home. Kate gets tickets to concerts and plays at the Atlanta Auditorium, and now she gets tickets to performances at the new Civic Center. Her parents sent her from Virginia to Atlanta, so she could take advantage of all the cultural things in Atlanta. They want Kate to be a well-rounded person, too."

Blanche had told me that Kate was from one of those "blue blood" families of the shipbuilding trade in Virginia. I had noticed that the neighbors called her "Tea Party." I asked one of them where she got that nickname. I was told that the day Kate moved in, Blanche and several of them were standing around on the balcony watching her remove items from her car. Kate, prim and proper, made several trips to and from the car. Each time, she would take dainty china cups and saucers up to her apartment. Blanche made the comment, "Another damn Tea Party." She had been called "Tea Party" by the neighbors since that day.

Kate went to Europe with her mother and aunt every year. Blanche said that last year, before I moved in next door to them, Kate was working at CDC. When her boss at CDC would not approve her vacation for the two weeks she planned to go to Europe, Kate resigned. Upon her return from Europe, Kate took a job downtown. Now that I worked in the building next door, we could have dinner and attend concerts and plays after work.

I said to Billy Joe, "And not only that, Kate works for a trade association just like I do. When they have meetings and banquets, I go over and help them get prepared. I even arranged for Al to do some of their printing."

I continued, "One day Al said, 'Am I going to have to start paying you a commission, too?' I would never let him pay me a commission, Billy Joe. He's already paying me too much."

After we hung up the phone, I thought about what Al had said concerning Billy Joe and me. One day Al was wrapping some of Kate's printed material when he said, "Looks like they're having a big shing-dig at the Marriott." I told him it would be the biggest yet, and that I didn't even know what I was going to wear.

Al knew that Kate's boss frequently sent me invitations to their receptions and banquets. Not only did I attend these functions with Kate, but I also had a few of my own company receptions and banquets that Mr. Green insisted I attend.

Al said, "Looks like you're a busy little lady. Socializing with all these big wheels and politicians in one world, and running with Billy Joe and his crowd in another. I guess you and Billy Joe do have a lot in common. You both know lawyers and politicians. It looks like you're both leading two lives and living in two worlds. I hope they don't ever collide."

"Al, you know the reason he runs with that crowd," I said. "When he got out of prison, he was only nineteen. He said that he felt as if some of his family, and a lot of other people in Overton, were skeptical of him. That 'crowd,' as you call it, welcomed him with open arms. That's the only reason he associates with them. So there! And the only lawyer we both know is Calhoun Johnson."

I remembered running into Calhoun Johnson at a reception recently after work. Cal looked at me and said, "Why am I not surprised to see you here? Janie, you do get around."

I had worked on a temporary assignment for Cal when I first moved to Atlanta. He was a member of a small law firm with three other lawyers. His secretary flew to California to be with her father who was very ill, and I filled in for her. After she had been gone three months, Cal told me his secretary's father had passed away, and she would be returning.

The next day, Cal asked me to have lunch with him. During lunch, Cal said that since his secretary would be returning, he didn't know what to do with me. He said, "Janie, we don't have enough space to keep you. There's not room for another single desk. And we can't go out and rent new office space just to accommodate a desk for you. But don't worry, I'll find you something else."

I was glad he took me to lunch to tell me. I felt like crying, but I would never cry in public.

In a way, I was relieved. This would make Mother happy. She had told me that Daddy didn't like it because I worked for Calhoun Johnson. She said that Daddy was having Milton Riggs, the deputy sheriff, check him out to see if he was the same Johnson that was running numbers in Atlanta.

Mother didn't have a clue what running numbers was, but I did. Lucky had told me that people would bet on numbers, and then they would check the Dow Jones close in the upper right-hand corner of the Atlanta Journal to see if they had won. I didn't see anything wrong with that.

One night, after I started working for Mr. Green, Billy Joe and I were leaving the Coach and Six. We ran into Cal at the entrance. He and Billy Joe shook hands and started talking.

Cal looked at me and did a double take. He said, "What a surprise to see you here, Janie! How have things been?" I told him everything was fine. While he was talking to Billy Joe, he kept glancing over at me.

When Cal was leaving, he said to Billy Joe, "I'll talk to you about it later." He glanced over at me again and said, "Good to see you, Janie." His eyebrow had the same question mark that Blanche's eyebrow would sometimes have. I wondered if that's what Al meant when he mentioned our "two worlds colliding."

Well, our two worlds couldn't collide when it came to politicians. I didn't believe Billy Joe and I knew any of the same ones. Billy Joe didn't even know a governor of Mississippi. But I did.

One Thursday, Mr. Green told me that a former governor was coming to Atlanta, and he asked me to wait at the office for the Governor to call. The Governor called before five o'clock and said, "Jane, tell Hiram I'm here at the Regency. He can call me here after his meeting, and we'll have dinner."

When Mr. Green called from his meeting, I said, "The Governor's here! At the Regency! He said for you to call him for dinner."

A few minutes later, I was closing up the office when Mr. Green called again. He asked, "Did the Governor give you his room number, Jane?"

I replied, "No, Mr. Green. Just call the front desk. They'll know the governor's room number."

Mr. Green sounded very upset. He said, "I did, Jane, and they don't even have him registered. How could you lose the Governor? You stay there, and maybe he'll call back."

I couldn't just sit there. I called and asked for every person I had ever talked to in the Banquets Department at the Regency. They had all gone home at five o'clock.

Finally, at six o'clock, the Governor called again. He told me he had not heard from Hiram yet and was wondering what had happened. He said he was getting hungry. I told the Governor what had happened, and then I said, "Boy, am I glad you called back. Mr. Green's real mad with me. He asked me, 'How could you lose the Governor?'"

The Governor laughed and laughed. He said, "Jane, you didn't lose me. The Regency lost me. Don't worry about Hiram. I'll take care of that."

The Governor gave me his room number, and I finally reached Mr. Green. He was still in that meeting at the Marriott. It was almost six-thirty by then, and I could go home.

Later, I asked Billy Joe if he knew any governor in Mississippi, since he was acquainted with so many politicians in Mississippi. He said he didn't. I told him I was glad, because I had lost the Governor at the Regency.

Billy Joe said, "Baby, how in the world could you lose a governor?"

When I told him, Billy Joe laughed as hard as the Governor had. I didn't think Mr. Green ever thought it was funny. He never mentioned it again after that night.

Later, I was thinking I should have told the Governor that Mr. Green was also mad because I had joined the Young Republicans. Maybe the Governor could have squared that one away, too.

Mr. Green was a staunch Democrat, and I asked him one day why he was so friendly with the Republicans. He told me it was his job, that he was a lobbyist.

But, there was one time when Mr. Green was real proud of me because I had joined the Young Republicans. He had to go to a reception down at one of the big bank buildings on a Friday night. He said he thought it would be a good idea for me to attend that one. It was a Republican affair, catered, with lots of food and plenty to drink. And, boy, were they drinking.

Billy Joe had told me that I should have only one drink at those functions, and for me to hold onto that one drink until it was time to leave. I didn't need Billy Joe telling me how to behave, but it was nice to know that he really cared. Sometimes he reminded me of Mr. Phillips— always giving advice.

I remembered the morning Mr. Phillips had a conflict in his schedule and asked me to attend a meeting as his representative. Before I left for the meeting, Mr. Phillips said, "Before you go, I'll give you a little advice. There will be carafes of coffee on the table. Pour one cup for yourself. Don't drink it all. You'll notice that the other ladies will have to excuse themselves to go to the ladies room. If you don't drink the coffee, you'll be able to sit there until they take a break." I had always remembered that advice whenever I was in a meeting.

When it was time to leave that night, Mr. Green told me a man with one of the banks on the north side of town was taking a cab home, and he would share it with me. I thought that was a good idea. I had shared many cabs with the people in my apartment building. Every time it rained, all the people going to work downtown would fill up several cabs.

Mr. Green walked over to me with a man about forty years old who was wearing a gray suit with a red tie. I had met him earlier that night. His name was Tom. Mr. Green told me that Tom had called the cab and was ready to go. I looked at my watch when we got in the elevator. It was ten o'clock. We walked out of the building, and the cab was waiting at the curb.

On the way to my apartment building, to make conversation, I asked Tom if he had children. He told me he had three of them and that his wife didn't work. When the cab pulled in at my apartment entrance, the driver got out and opened my door.

Tom got out, too, and started paying the driver. I asked Tom if he lived in my building. He said, "No, I thought we could have a nightcap, and then I would call another cab." I wondered what his wife would think about that!

I told him I didn't have anything except coffee and Cokes. I knew what a nightcap was. I told Tom that it was about time for me to wake up my boyfriend anyway. I said, "He works on the night shift, you know, and he has to be at work in two hours. He's upstairs taking a nap."

Tom acted real mad and got back in the cab. I had never seen a Republican get that mad. The cab driver gave me a big smile.

The next night when Billy Joe called, I told him about Tom. Billy Joe thought it was the funniest thing he had ever heard. He said, "Baby, you'll probably be looking for another job real soon, but at least I can give you credit for having good sense."

On Monday, when I walked into my office at exactly nine o'clock, I saw that Mr. Green was already there. He was on the phone. I heard the receiver hit the cradle when he hung up the phone. He said in a loud voice, "Jane, you didn't tell me that Billy Joe lived with you."

I replied, "He doesn't, Mr. Green."

Mr. Green said, "Then what was he doing there Friday night?"

I replied, "He wasn't, Mr. Green. Billy Joe was out of town."

I heard him slamming objects around on his desk. Mr. Green didn't speak to me the rest of the day. I was glad he had to go out of town for the remainder of the week. I thought it was rude not to speak to your own secretary.

Mr. Green was so different from Mr. Phillips. Some days, Mr. Phillips would be in a quiet mood, but he spoke to me every day. And if someone like Tom had wanted to share a cab with me, Mr. Phillips would have said, "Not on your life."

One day Harry told Billy Joe that with all my connections, I could have his girls turning more tricks at the Marriott than he could. Billy Joe said, "Watch it! Watch it!" At the time, I didn't know what Harry meant, but I knew it was not a good thing if it made Billy Joe say a double, "Watch it!"

Later, I asked Billy Joe what Harry meant. When he told me, I was baffled. I had never met a pimp before. And I had never dreamed that one would look like Harry. Except for the two times I had seen him in a suit, Harry wore plain slacks and a short-sleeved sports shirt. In my mind, a pimp would be wearing a loud suit, sunglasses, and a hat. I didn't know where I came up with that idea, but that's what I visualized when I heard the word "pimp." I told Billy Joe what I thought, and he said, "Baby, pimps are normal people—like everybody else."

I replied, "Pimps, normal? That's an oxymoron, Billy Joe."

He laughed and said, "Ah, step it!" That was another phrase Billy Joe used a lot when he was amused. It was as if to say, "You've got me there. I can't top that!"

12.

In His Corner

I had arrived home from work and was packing a bag. Billy Joe and I were driving over to Augusta. As I threw my swimsuit in the bag, Billy Joe rang the doorbell. I opened the door, and he came in grinning from ear to ear.

"What is it?" I asked. He kept grinning.

Finally, he said, "Dang, Baby, it's no wonder you act the way you do! You had me convinced that you were the black sheep of your family. And today I found out the truth!"

"What are you talking about?" I asked.

"The truth about who's the real spoiled brat in your family!" He started laughing. Then he added, "I stopped by to see your Aunt Maggie today."

Her name was Mary Margaret, but everybody called her Maggie. Even as a child, I was allowed to call her "Maggie," too. She knew it made me feel grown up when I didn't have to say "Aunt Maggie." She had five children and another one on the way. She was Lucky's sister and my mother's sister. She was tough; she was sweet. I was her favorite niece.

When I was in the first grade, Maggie bought me two dresses. One had pockets. In one of the pockets, there was a Cinderella watch.

When I was thirteen, Maggie had a new baby. I spent the entire summer with her, taking care of the baby and washing and ironing. That was the summer she taught me to drive. Of course, she wouldn't allow me to drive on the main highway until I was fifteen. By then, I was an expert driver, or so I thought.

I spent the weekends with her when I was a teenager. There were always children around. And we were all happy.

Every time I returned home from being at Maggie's, my family treated me differently. They said that I had an "attitude." Well, maybe I did.

Billy Joe and Maggie had met over the phone. One night he arrived while I was talking with Maggie on the phone, so that's how they were introduced. She had him laughing, even then.

Billy Joe looked at me and said, "It surely does explain a lot to me—just meeting your Aunt Maggie made me feel special, too." He told me about the children running in and out, and that there was one little girl he called "Dimples" because her dimples were as deep as Grand Canyon.

He started laughing again and said, "Maggie told me not to worry about what your daddy thought about me. That she was the one I had to worry about. And all this time, I've been worrying about Lucky. I didn't know you had so many people in your corner, Baby. I wish I had people in my corner."

I thought, "You do, Billy Joe. You do."

Billy Joe asked me if I was ready to go. I didn't know why he had to go, but he said we were bound for Augusta. As we started out the door, he said, "If you're hungry, grab something to tide you over until we get there. I told Matthew we would go to eat with them." I didn't need anything to eat; I could wait.

It was a long drive, but Billy Joe was driving. He usually drove, except in broad daylight, after he discovered that my night vision was very poor. One evening at dusk, he was driving down a two-lane highway when I said, "Watch that dog!"

He turned and looked at me. "What dog?" he asked.

I said, "Oh, I thought that was a dog. It's difficult to see at dusk. I was afraid it was going to run in front of the car. I didn't want you to hit it."

"Baby," he said, "Maybe you'd better see the eye doctor. If you can't tell the difference between a dog and a mailbox, I'm beginning to worry about you." I knew it would be dusk before we reached Augusta, and that's why he was the one driving.

I wore the brown mini-dress that had the underpants to match. I remembered the Saturday afternoon Billy Joe picked me up to go see *Georgy Girl*. He had said, "Before we go to the movie, I want to run down to the Snooty-Hooty. That's a new clothing shop located between the Atlanta Federal Building and the Federal Reserve. I was down at The Magic Mirror yesterday, and Pete was telling me that they had some real cute clothes. He bought several outfits for Susan there. I want to check it out."

We parked in the parking lot at the Palmer Building and Davis Brothers Cafeteria and walked across the street to the Snooty-Hooty. And they did have some cute clothes. Billy Joe picked out a brown mini-dress and a striped jacket with matching shorts for me to try on. The mini-dress was made of voile and had a thin cotton lining. The jacket and shorts were green, red and white striped. The shorts had a cuff and came to about four inches above the knee. Billy Joe chose a red sleeveless turtleneck sweater to match. I liked the outfit, but I couldn't stand wearing a turtleneck. When I tried it on, Billy Joe said, "I really do like that. The turtleneck looks real good on you. I never see you wearing a turtleneck." I guessed I would be wearing a turtleneck, since he was already paying for both outfits.

As we headed to Augusta, I said, "Billy Joe, you know this brown mini-dress is one of my favorites. Well, today at work, I was on the elevator going up to my floor, and there were two women on there with me. They work on my floor, but I don't really know them. They were behind me when I got on, and I heard one of them say, 'I wish you'd look at that.' I knew they were talking about this mini-dress. But I didn't care. Mr. Green likes it fine, and young people wear them to work. It's just that these old women over forty years old don't have one, don't you think?"

Billy Joe said, "They probably don't. That one is not too short, anyway. And just because you work doesn't mean you have to wear old women's clothes. They're jealous because you're so young, Baby. Don't worry so much about what other people think."

Before we arrived in Augusta, Billy Joe told me that Matthew had been a successful politician in Mississippi until he was found guilty of fraud and sent to prison. While in prison, Matthew did not want his wife to be even more humiliated by having to visit him there, so he asked her not to see him. Their marriage fell apart during that time, and when Matthew was released, they were divorced. Sherry had worked for Matthew and, somehow, had ended up married to him shortly after his divorce. And then Little Matthew was born. Billy Joe said that Matthew had been selling stocks and bonds since his release from prison. I wondered how he could get a license to sell stocks and bonds if he had been in prison. Working with Mr. Phillips had taught me a little about stockbrokers and investments.

Billy Joe told me that Sherry would go to the bus station and catch the next bus home every time she and Matthew had a spat. He said, "To top it all, she is always the one causing the spat. Matthew does everything to please her, and she is never happy with anything. I wish he would leave her at home. Every time I go past a bus station, I want to look in the window and see if she's sitting there waiting for a bus." I knew I would, too, after he told me that.

It was eight-thirty when we arrived at the motel. Billy Joe checked in and called Matthew's room. We met them on the stairway and, after introductions, drove to a restaurant that specialized in hamburgers, steak and chicken. Little Matthew was a rough and tough little boy. But he was good that night, and he went to sleep before we had finished our meal.

On Saturday, Billy Joe told me that Matthew had some business to take care of and that we would meet Sherry and Little Matthew at the pool.

When we arrived at the pool, Sherry was taking pictures of Little Matthew. Then she took one of Billy Joe and me. Billy Joe said, "Give me the camera, Sherry, and I'll take one of you and Little Matthew."

She handed him the camera. Billy Joe held it up, hit the wrong button and the film fell out. He said, "Look what I've done now, Sherry. I can't believe that happened."

On the way back to the rooms, Billy Joe looked at Sherry and said, "Sorry about your film. I'll get you some more."

He turned to me after she went in her room and said, "I don't know why she brought that camera. She knows not to take pictures of you— or me either. What was that woman thinking?"

We met them again for dinner that night. Matthew had been working on a business deal all day, so he still had on a business suit. He really looked like a politician in that suit. Matthew was very polished. I didn't think he and Sherry made a good match. She seemed to be a good mother, but she whined all the time to Matthew.

We didn't see Matthew and Sherry again. Early the next morning, Billy Joe and I drove back home.

On the way home, I told Billy Joe that the names Big Matthew and Little Matthew reminded me of Big Bee and Little Bee, and Big Dice and Little Dice. Billy Joe said, "Yes, Little Bee was a friend of mine in school. We used to hang out together all the time. He was a good football player."

I asked Billy Joe if he ever ate any of the tomato soup that Little Bee's mother made. He couldn't remember what he ate back then. I told him it was real good. She added milk to it and called it "cream of tomato." No one in my family added milk to tomato soup.

I told Billy Joe that I ate at Little Bee's house sometimes because his sister was a friend of mine. After school we would go to her house, listen to records and make fudge or pizza. I said, "One night we were watching television with her dad, Big Bee. The contestants were giving their names to Groucho Marx. Big Bee said that if he had to go on Groucho's show, he would be so nervous that he wouldn't even remember his real name. He was afraid he would say, 'Uh, Bee.' Every time I saw Big Bee after that, I thought about Groucho Marx."

I was thinking that if I had to be on that show, I would probably tell Groucho my name was "Uh, Baby." Billy Joe called me "Baby" so much that I was beginning to think it was my real name.

Billy Joe said, "I wonder what Big Dice and Little Dice are doing now." I told him I didn't know about his brother, but that Little Dice had worked at the gas station on Monroe Drive.

"I don't think he's there now, but I know that when I was working for Mr. Phillips over a year ago, I stopped in to get gas, and Little Dice came out to pump it. When he saw me sitting there in the car, Little Dice said, 'What in the world are you doing way up here?' I told him I worked down the street, and I lived off Lenox near Cheshire Bridge. He was always happy to see me when I drove up," I said.

"One afternoon I stopped to get gas and I had to write a check. Now you remember, Billy Joe, I didn't make as much money as I do now, so I told Little Dice to give me three dollar's worth because I didn't get paid until Friday, and I was running short on cash.

"Little Dice said, 'That's okay, Jane. I'll go ahead and fill it up. I can hold your check until you get paid.'

"After that, every time I was running short on cash, I would tell him, 'Hold that check!' And he would. It's nice to have friends from home, don't you think?"

Billy Joe reached over and squeezed my hand.

Billy Joe was almost six years older than I. When he was a teenager in Overton, there was no place to go except the pool room. That's where the boys hung out. Of course, girls were not allowed in the pool room, and I was too young to be going anywhere.

The pool room was probably one reason Billy Joe didn't use profanity. Gus, the owner, served hot dogs and brunswick stew. The teenage boys would eat hot dogs and play pool. I had heard that if any one of them ever used profanity, Gus would hit them with a pool stick! And there was not one thing they could do about it. In Overton, parents allowed any adult in town to correct their children if they saw them doing anything wrong. The parents would have sided with Gus, so the boys learned not to use profanity.

There was nowhere else to go in Overton, and since the boys stayed in the pool room so much of the time, profanity was not a part of their vocabulary.

By the time I was a teenager, we had Garrison's Restaurant. It was a teenager's second home. Mrs. Garrison enjoyed having us there. We could play the jukebox as loud as we wanted, and she never complained. The menu consisted of meats, vegetables, hamburgers, steaks, and just about anything you could name. We usually ate hamburgers and chocolate or lemon pie.

If there were any of us who didn't have money, we could order a "pine float." That was what we called a toothpick and a glass of water. I told Billy Joe about the time Gregg Jenkins didn't have but a dime. He asked Mrs. Garrison what he could get for a dime. She told him an onion sandwich. He looked at her out of the corner of his eye and asked, "Could you put mustard on it?"

On a Tuesday night, two weeks after we had been in Augusta, Billy Joe called me from there. He asked if I would take a flight down after work. Even though he would probably be home on Saturday, he said he wanted to see me for dinner. He told me that he and Matthew were trying to wind up a business deal.

After work, I took a cab to the airport and flew to Augusta. I knew I would fly back that night. I had to be at work the next morning. Billy Joe met me at the airport. He was wearing a business suit, and he told me he had been working with Matthew in his stocks and bonds business.

We had a nice dinner, just the two of us. The tablecloths in the small restaurant were white linen, and the flatware was silver plated. The waiter brought a rose to our table. The card read "Love."

After dinner, Billy Joe drove me back to the airport. As soon as we got there, he walked over to a phone booth to make a call. Then he motioned me over, and while I was standing in the doorway of the booth, he took out a bulky envelope and placed it in my handbag. He said, "Baby, these are some important papers. Take this envelope home and put it in one of your shoeboxes. Hold it for me."

I said, "Okay." I had worked for lawyers, so I knew all about holding on to important papers. I also figured there was money in that envelope. Money had a "cushiony" feel; important papers had a "crisp" feel.

On Tuesday of the following week, Billy Joe called me at work. He said he had a surprise for me, and he would pick me up around eight o'clock to go to dinner. But first he had to go home, take a shower and change clothes. I didn't know why he was waiting so late to get started.

When he arrived, he had a big smile on his face as he told me he had taken a job—a real job. It was with a bonding company. I was thinking that perhaps his working with Matthew in Augusta, along with my occasional hints, had motivated Billy Joe to take a real job.

That day had been his second day at work. It had also been his second day of headaches. He said, "Baby, I don't know how long I can work there; I can't live with a headache every day."

I was excited about his new job. Over dinner, I asked him to tell me about it. And he did. He went on and on with some of the funniest stories I had ever heard about people getting out of jail—things that had happened during the past two days. He seemed as excited about the job as I was. Our conversation was quite different and made for an enjoyable evening. I was happy for Billy Joe.

On Thursday night, Billy Joe came by and brought food for dinner. As we sat at the dining room table, I asked him about his day at work. He told me he couldn't keep the job. His headaches had been worse on Wednesday and Thursday, and he didn't like being tied down all day. He said, "I'm sorry to disappoint you, Baby."

My heart dropped. I had never felt so disappointed. Not for myself, but for Billy Joe.

There was one thing to be said for Billy Joe. He made no excuses—no explanations, no defense—nothing. He had told me one time that there was no reason to hash and re-hash. "What's done is done," he had said. At the time, he was referring to my move downtown as I tried to explain my reasons for moving there. I learned early on that when Billy Joe ended a subject, it was ended. We never mentioned a "real job" again.

13.

The Piano

My job downtown was a delight, and I was enjoying being on a bowling team. Several people who worked on my floor had asked me to join their league. I couldn't bowl well, but they didn't seem to mind. After bowling on Tuesday and Thursday nights, we usually stopped by the piano bar at the Rodeway Inn on 14th Street. We would have a drink and sit at the piano bar and sing.

I was getting excited about music. After several years of piano lessons in Overton, and not much practice since, I decided it was time to buy a piano. There was a place down on Peters Street running a big sale. One afternoon at five o'clock, I drove down to take a look. There was an ebony spinet for only $795.00 that I had to have.

When I got home that evening, I remembered Daddy saying "The only place you can find a helping hand is at the end of your arm." So I picked up the phone and let that hand at the end of my arm dial Lucky, the best uncle in the whole world.

I told Lucky I needed some advice about a piano. I gave him all the financing arrangements, as quoted to me, and asked how much he thought my down payment should be. Lucky said, "Don't pay finance charges. I guarandamntee you'll go broke doing that! Drop by here Thursday night and I'll give you the money if you've just got to have the damn thing." I was hoping he would say that.

I could remember when I was a teenager; Lucky would give me a $100 bill to go to the store for him. He never asked for the change, and I never gave it to him. One day Lucky was cutting the grass when a neighbor walked over and asked to borrow a garden hose. The neighbor said he should go buy one, they were just $4.00. Lucky said, "$4.00? Hell, I thought a garden hose cost $100.00." He looked at me and grinned.

While I had Lucky on the phone, he asked how Billy Joe was doing. I told him I thought Billy Joe was still in Biloxi. Lucky said, "It would be a good idea for you to stay out of Biloxi for a while." I asked why and he replied, "Don't ask me why; just damn do what I say."

He sounded real mad about it, so I said, "Okay."

Then he said, "I'll see you Thursday night at seven o'clock; don't get out." Lucky owned a bar and grill. His patrons were a little "rough around the edges," so he didn't like for me to come inside. Somehow, he always knew when I drove up.

Lacking the patience to wait for the following Thursday night, I had the piano delivered on Saturday. The two-year contract I signed had an addendum so that I could pay cash with no finance charges within the first thirty days. I knew I was doing what my grandmother, Mimi, would call "counting chickens before they hatched," but Lucky had never let me down.

The following Tuesday night, my mother called to tell me that there had been a fight at Lucky's bar and grill. Lucky tried to break it up and was shot by a stray bullet. He didn't survive the wound. I tried to pretend she had not said it. Not my Lucky, the best uncle in the whole wide world! No one cared about me as much as Lucky. I didn't see him often, and usually it was when he called me to come pick up money for my retirement. He knew I spent it. And it wasn't the money; I just wanted him to be there. I didn't care about his money. I could make my own money. He always said I was a survivor!

I returned from the funeral home late Wednesday night. Billy Joe called me after I was in bed. He had read the three-column article about Lucky in the papers. My mother was embarrassed. There were so many things she did not know about Lucky. The paper said he had been a gambler, a bookie, and a loan shark. I knew Lucky would lend money to people who couldn't get it from the bank, but I didn't know it was against the law. Billy Joe told me he was sorry about all the stuff in the paper.

I told Billy Joe that I couldn't believe how Lucky's life had turned out. Lucky had been a happily married man six years ago when he was married to Gina. He had a good job and a nice home. He would work in the yard all weekend and play in the kiddie pool with Anna, their daughter.

Anna had a stubborn streak and had picked up some of Lucky's profanity. When I was living there, I had Southern Memorial Day off in April. Gina had to work, so I stayed home with Anna. Late that afternoon, Anna and I were to take the bus downtown, meet Gina, and go shopping. We got dressed and walked the three blocks to the bus stop. When the bus arrived, the driver stopped and opened the door. Anna stomped her little foot and said, "I'm not getting on that damn bus."

Shocked by her outburst, I begged her to get on. Then I had to coax her by promising to buy her another Barbie doll. She finally got on the bus, but she sat in her seat and watched me out of the corner of her eye. That sweet little thing was gloating. I could have choked her.

I said to Billy Joe, "Something happened, and Lucky changed—not toward me, but I could see a difference in the way he acted. He quit his good job and opened a bar and grill."

That was when I informed Billy Joe that Lucky had told me a long time ago if anything ever happened to him, he wanted me to know there was plenty for my retirement in the attic of The Red Barn. It was located on the south side of town and had once been a tavern. Lucky had a long-term lease on the property, so he was still paying the lease even though the building was vacant. But Lucky also told me not to go there alone. I had no idea what was in the attic, but I told Billy Joe that it could be pills. I had heard someone say one time that Lucky had enough pills to sink a battleship. And Lucky had told me not to ever take pills—not even if the doctor prescribed them. Lucky had said that most of the dope addicts on the street started out taking prescription drugs. Billy

Joe said that whatever was there probably was not there now if Lucky told me this a long time ago. I didn't know why I even mentioned it to Billy Joe.

Lucky liked Billy Joe, but he really didn't want me to see him. I could tell by a conversation they had on the phone. One night Lucky called when Billy Joe was there, and asked to talk with him. I handed the phone to Billy Joe and went back to the kitchen. I could hear Billy Joe saying things like, "I know, I understand, don't worry, she'll be okay with me, I promise."

Billy Joe and I ended our phone conversation, and I tried to go to sleep. My mind was turning over and over with thoughts of Lucky and all the fun things we had done.

I asked Mimi one time how Lucky got that name. She told me that as a teenager, Lucky and a friend had driven to Griffin one Saturday afternoon. They took in a movie and were on the way to get an ice cream cone at the Spinning Wheel. Lucky stopped at the train track, but being the daredevil he was, he thought he could beat the train. He almost did, but the train hit the back bumper of the car. The doctors had to operate on Lucky's elbow and insert a pin. The friend was okay, and the car was repaired, but Lucky would always have a pin in his elbow. The neighbors said he was "lucky" he didn't get killed. That's when they started calling him Lucky. Now they were probably saying that his luck had run out.

I remembered my visit during the summer of 1958. On a Saturday afternoon I was sweeping the driveway, Gina and Anna were in the kiddie pool, and Lucky was cutting the grass. He had finished using the riding mower and was doing the trim work around the shrubbery with the push mower. The motor kept going dead. After starting it several times, I heard Lucky say, "Damn it to hell!"

As he went inside, he said to me, "Get your pocketbook and let's go." I went inside and grabbed my bag. He came out buttoning his shirt and then he crammed his money clip into his pocket. He shouted out to

Gina in the backyard, "We're going down to Rich's to get a lawn mower. Jane's driving." We got in the car; the keys were in the ignition.

I was only fifteen and had a learner's license, and Lucky wanted me to drive downtown. He said that was the only way I would learn. When we got to Rich's Store for Homes, Lucky said, "Let me out here. You circle the block until you see me. I'll be on this corner."

As he opened the door to get out, I said, "What if the police stop me? I don't have a real driver's license. It's just a learner's license."

He said, "Well, hell. Just tell them you're learning." He got out, closed the door, and drew circles in the air with his finger. I saw him laughing all the way to the entrance of the Store for Homes. He was having a good time.

I was driving Lucky's red 1958 Chevrolet Impala convertible with four-in-the-floor. The top was down, and people were looking at me. But I wasn't nervous. I had to go up a hill, circling the block. Traffic was heavy that Saturday afternoon, and cars were lined up at the traffic light on the way up the hill. They would inch along, and I had no trouble doing that with the four-speed transmission. Lucky had taught me to drive it without killing the motor, and I never made the car jump and jerk. It was smooth sailing. I knew exactly how to coordinate the clutch and the accelerator. I could hold the car in position, move up six inches, hold my position, and do it again—without having to touch the brake. I had told Lucky that it would wear out the clutch, but he said, "Hell, look how much you're saving on brakes."

I had made several trips around the block and finally I saw Lucky standing on the corner. He had a huge box that he had set on the sidewalk. I drove up and stopped. He picked up the box containing the lawn mower and placed it in the back seat.

As he got in the car, he said, "H. A." I knew that meant "Haul Ass." Gina wouldn't allow Lucky to say "Haul Ass" in Anna's presence, so Lucky had started saying "H. A."

One time I was riding home with them, and Lucky was "hauling ass" up the South Freeway. Gina said, "Slow this car down."

Lucky replied, "Hell, I'm down to 80."

It's no wonder I had a heavy foot. Lucky had told me that I only needed to know two speeds: full speed ahead and stop. I drifted off to sleep that night thinking how fast Lucky had driven.

The funeral was on Thursday afternoon. Late Thursday night, The Red Barn burned to the ground. Fire inspectors said it was arson. Of course, there was another big write-up in the paper. I would never know what was in the attic, and Billy Joe said it was for the best.

14.

Bowling Green

Billy Joe called and asked me if I would like to ride up to Kentucky. He said he had to make a business transaction there. I told him I would. I couldn't imagine what kind of business he had in Kentucky.

I was in such a hurry getting packed that I dropped my bottle of Holiday Magic makeup. Not only did the bottle break, but also there was makeup all over the bathroom tile. I didn't have time to clean up that mess, so I left a soggy towel on it.

Billy Joe arrived, assessed the damage and said, "Baby, you can't leave the floor like that. I'll do it now." He cleaned the floor while I finished stuffing my overnight bag. I grabbed a ball of red knitting yarn and needles and crammed them in the bag.

When we got to the car, Billy Joe opened my door, so I assumed he was driving. In the daylight hours, he usually ushered me around to the driver's side and opened that door for me. I was glad I didn't have to drive. I had other plans on this trip. I said, "Wait! Before you put that bag in the trunk, I need to take out my knitting yarn." He held the bag open and I removed the yarn and needles.

He said, "I hope that's not going to be a sweater for me; you know I don't wear red."

And he was right. Billy Joe wore black, white, gray, brown, tan, beige, navy, light blue, and sometimes pale yellow. He told me he wore those colors in 100% Alpaca wool sweaters in the winter. The weather was still warm, but fall fashions were on display in the stores. We were looking at the sweaters one night in Muses when he said that Alpaca was the best—then he proceeded to tell me how they would take these baby alpacas, feed them well, and when they grew up, they would shear them to make Alpaca wool. I didn't even call the Atlanta Public Library to check that one out.

When he got in the car and drove off, I said, "Billy Joe, I'm not even making a sweater. I'm making a knitted bag that will cushion and protect my makeup. I just can't afford to break another bottle."

He said, "Baby, when you dropped it, were you using it?"

I replied, "Yes, and it slipped out of my hand."

He laughed out loud. Then he said, "How do you think that red bag would have helped, if you were already using it? It would have been out of the bag when you dropped it." I had not thought about that. I kept knitting.

We stopped and had breakfast. He drove on. We stopped and had lunch. He drove on. When he drove, he talked. When he talked, I listened.

He started talking about Tony. "I don't know what his trouble is up here. The attorney called and told me to bring money and we would discuss it. I didn't know what else to do. I can't leave Tony in jail."

"In jail?" I asked. I wanted to know why, but I never asked Billy Joe questions about things like that. I had to wait until he wanted to tell me something. And sometimes, I was sorry he told me.

"Yeah, in jail, and I don't know why. Pimping is just a misdemeanor in Georgia. All I know is that the attorney wanted me to come up. Or rather, he wanted someone with money to come up. I don't know what he's done that's so bad we couldn't send the money," he said. "But that's okay; it will give us a little trip, won't it?"

I didn't answer. I was thinking about Tony being a pimp. So that explained it. The first time I met him, I thought he was a salesman. And I had been right.

We drove on. I kept knitting. We were already in Bowling Green. Billy Joe was driving around the square. He pointed out the park and said, "That's Fountain Square Park. I'll bet you're wondering how it got that name."

He paused, then continued, "I know you are, so I'll tell you. It's a park on the square and it has a cast iron fountain. Do you believe that?"

"How do you know the fountain is cast iron?" I asked.

He laughed and said, "Trust me."

As he drove on past the Park, I thought, "Well, why not." If Billy Joe and Big Red wanted to fill their minds with history, geography, baseball and football statistics, that was fine with me. I had no need for that information. I certainly didn't plan to bet $100.00 with Tony that I could answer five out of any six questions he asked. Billy Joe had made that bet and won. Big Red also won. He had bet Tony $100.00 that Billy Joe could do it. I was not interested in all that trivia. Clothes, shoes and fabrics were my interests, plus knitting the red bag.

I was checking to see if the old bottle of makeup I had brought would fit the bag before I finished sewing it together. It did, but I noticed that the little makeup left in the bottle had dried out. I said, "I wish I had ordered more of this Holiday Magic. But I had a new bottle, and I didn't think I would need two of them. I don't know what I'm going to do for makeup. This has dried out."

Billy Joe said, "Don't worry, we'll stop at the store and get you some more."

"But I have to get this from someone who sells it. Distributors sell it from their homes. I can't wear just any makeup; it makes my skin turn orange," I replied.

Billy Joe didn't say anything. In a few minutes, he pulled over to a parking space in front of a phone booth, turned to me and said, "Baby, I've got to make a phone call." He was on the phone several times. I saw him looking up numbers in the book. Then he hung up the phone and started back to the car with a big grin on his face.

He got in the car and said, "I've got some time to kill before I see the attorney, but there's somewhere else we need to go anyway." Then he drove off.

He drove several blocks, turned left, and then drove two miles, turned right, then left. He was repeating directions as he drove. Then he turned into a driveway. He pulled out his money clip, handed me a wad of bills and said, "Go in there and get a bottle of makeup. This is the home of the Holiday Magic distributor for Bowling Green!"

I was flabbergasted! He must be the only man in the world who paid attention. I started smiling, took the money, and went up to the front door. He rolled down the window and hollered out, "Be sure you get the size that fits your new red bag!" I could hear him laughing as he rolled up the window.

He drove to the jail and met the attorney at five o'clock. I stayed in the car. He was gone for about forty-five minutes. When he returned to the car, he had nothing to say for a long time on the way out of town.

After we had been on the freeway a while, Billy Joe found a Holiday Inn. He said that would be as good as anything we could find on the freeway. The lady at the desk asked Billy Joe if he had reservations. He replied, "I have a few, but I want to stay here anyway." He glanced at me and winked. His comment was a good indication that he was feeling better. The lady was at a loss as to what to say to him, so she handed him the registration form.

After checking in, we had dinner in the restaurant downstairs. Billy Joe made very little conversation at dinner. It was obvious to me that he was in his "thinking mode," so I asked no questions. Tony's predicament was not mentioned, and I would never know what happened.

The next morning, we headed home. I was glad Billy Joe was in a talkative mood again. He drove and talked, drove and talked.

Suddenly, Billy Joe stopped talking. Then he said, "Baby, are you asleep?" I answered, "No, why?"

"I thought you were," he said. "You're mighty quiet."

"I'm just listening to you, Billy Joe."

He smiled and said, "I've been talking for 100 miles. And you haven't said a word. I'll bet you haven't paid attention to anything I said. Have you paid attention to the scenery? Did you notice all those green pastures, white fences and horses?"

I replied, "No, Billy Joe, I'm just leaning back, watching the windshield and listening to you."

He reached over, took my hand, and squeezed it. I loved to hear Billy Joe talk. Most people thought he was a quiet, shy person, but when it was just the two of us, he wouldn't shut up—unless he was thinking, of course.

Billy Joe was a complex person, but he was not complicated. I understood him and he was aware of that. I always knew when to talk and when to listen. I couldn't say that was true when I was around other people.

Then Billy Joe said, "Baby, do you feel okay?" I nodded my head.

"You usually talk 90 miles a minute. That's faster than I can drive," he said. "If I drove 90 miles a minute, how long would it take us to get home?"

"I don't even know where we are, Billy Joe, but I would guess approximately an hour and three minutes," I replied.

"We're not that far from home, Baby. Couldn't possibly be. How do you figure it would take that long?"

"I'm just guessing," I said, "but I think approximately one hour to eat and three minutes to get home."

"In that case," he said, "you're approximately correct. Why did you figure an hour to eat?"

"I know you, Billy Joe. And it's about time for you to be hungry again," I laughed.

"Do you realize, Miss Moss, that you know me better than anyone else on earth?"

"Probably so," I said.

15.

Vegas

Billy Joe met me at the airport in Vegas on a Saturday. I was relieved to see that he was in his own car. As long as I had known him, I had flown while he had driven. I said, "Billy Joe, you missed a good flight. Why don't you ever fly with me?" He looked at me and laughed. Then he said, "Baby, as long as they sell cars and gas, I don't plan to fly again."

Billy Joe drove us straight to the Hilton so that I could refresh my makeup, comb my hair, and change clothes. Then we went downstairs to the front door and stepped into a cab. After driving around town and down what Billy Joe called "The Strip," the cab driver dropped us off at Caesar's Palace, one of the newer places. There we ran into Harry, Renee and Tony. I looked around, but I didn't see Eve. I asked where Eve was and Renee told me that she was at work. I certainly didn't want to get into that subject again. I knew what her job was. Soon they moved on, so I didn't have to make anymore conversation with them.

I was glad to move away from Harry. I didn't want to be near Harry in Vegas, not after what he had said to me at Shoney's that morning a few weeks ago. Billy Joe and I had breakfast at Shoney's across from Broadview Plaza on a Saturday morning. As we were leaving, Tony's silver El Dorado drove up and Harry got out of the car. Billy Joe had told me that Tony paid cash for that El Dorado as soon as he was released from prison for burglarizing one of the large downtown department stores. He didn't say which one, and I wondered if he was just kidding me again.

Tony drove off, leaving Harry standing in the parking lot. Harry hurried over to Billy Joe and said, "I was hoping I would catch you here. We need to go to DeKalb County."

Billy Joe told Harry he would have to take me home first—that there was no way he was taking me with them. Harry pointed toward the east and said, "DeKalb's that way, and we need to be there now." Then, looking at me, Harry said, "Remind me when we get to Vegas to leave you out in the desert." I backed away from him. That's when I realized Harry was a formidable foe.

The muscle in Billy Joe's jaw got tight. I could see the vein in his neck pounding. He was livid! I immediately spoke up and said, "Don't worry, Billy Joe, I can take a cab."

He replied, "If you don't mind, Baby." He handed me a $100 bill for the cab.

I remembered the first time Billy Joe handed me a $100 bill for cab fare. I said, "This is too much. Don't you have a ten?"

Billy Joe had replied, "Baby, when I give you cab fare, don't question how much. Besides, it's a hot day and you might want to stop for an ice cream cone or something." Then he smiled and winked at me.

So I had never said another word about how much a cab would cost. And I had probably saved enough from the cab fares he gave me to buy my own cab, if I had wanted one.

When Billy Joe and I had taken a cab from the Hilton to Caesar's Palace that night, I asked him why we didn't take his car. He said we would be going to several places and he preferred to take a cab in Vegas. "And besides," he said, "the wind would mess up your hair walking from the parking lot."

I was glad to be taking a cab. I would not want to be left at the door while Billy Joe parked the car. He was aware that I felt self conscious in some circumstances. Sometimes I would meet him at clubs after work, and I never had to look for him. I wouldn't see him beforehand, but immediately after entering the door, Billy Joe, lithe as a panther, would appear at my side.

While at Caesar's Palace, there were three men I had not seen before who walked over and spoke to Billy Joe. They told him how good it was to see him again. Billy Joe forgot his Southern manners. He didn't even introduce me to those people.

Jamie was there. He asked me if I still had that Mustang. There were two or three others I had met previously. They acknowledged my presence, and they even remembered my name. But I was not introduced to anyone I had not already met.

Then I looked across the room and saw Slot. I said, "Billy Joe, there's Slot. What's he doing here?"

"They gave him a one-way ticket out of Atlanta and told him not to come back. He lives and works here now, Baby. He and Jean got married, and Jean still works at the airline. She lives in Atlanta, but she gets to fly down here all the time."

I would recognize Slot anywhere. I think it was the haircut. It was stylish on men then, but it looked like someone had placed a bowl on his head and cut around it. He had a "Beatles" look that accentuated his big round eyes. Billy Joe still wore his jet black hair close cropped with short sideburns. Billy Joe looked handsome and rugged.

I had learned from Billy Joe that Slot got his name after he won a large sum of money playing the slot machines in Vegas. We used to meet Slot and Jean, along with Lex and Annette, downtown at the Knight's Table on Sunday evenings for dinner. The building that housed the Knight's Table had once been the Ship Ahoy, but it had closed. Then there was the Knight's Table.

Lex and Annette were Billy Joe's friends, too. We would meet the four of them occasionally for dinner on Sunday nights. Lex was a retired race car driver who worked at an automobile dealership. He liked to have Billy Joe and me come over and watch all the old race films with him. Annette was a talkative, vivacious blonde with a winning personality.

During election time, she was an active volunteer in local political campaigns. She was the perfect hostess.

When we went to their house to watch the racing films, we would cook steaks on the grill. Lex had to have a can of pinto beans with his steak. They were both comical. Lex would carry a bag of jalapeno peppers in his shirt pocket, and no matter where we ate, he would take them out and place them on the table.

I remembered the first time I met Slot and Jean. After dinner that night, we walked over to the Rialto and saw *Bonnie and Clyde*. I liked the movie, but it was very scary. We walked back to the parking lot, and while waiting for the attendants to bring the cars, Lex said, "Let's do this again next Sunday."

Billy Joe replied, "Sounds good to me, how about you, Slot?"

Slot just shrugged his shoulders and said, "Okay, if I'm here next Sunday."

We met Lex and Annette the next Sunday, but Slot and Jean were not there. Annette said that sometimes Jean would be on a flight on Sunday, or Slot would be out of town, so they didn't show up every time. But they had shown up several times after that night.

The last time I saw Slot, Billy Joe and I met him in a bar in Decatur. We sat at the bar. Billy Joe sat in the middle so he and Slot could discuss business. I couldn't hear what they were talking about, but Billy Joe gave him some traveler's checks.

It had been a while since Billy Joe had mentioned Slot, and that's why I was so surprised to see him in Vegas. It was a busy casino and I wanted to go over and speak to him, but Billy Joe said, "No, he's working now. We'll see him later. Let's get you some quarters."

I enjoyed playing the slot machines. Billy Joe would give me cups of quarters, and sometimes he would go to the blackjack tables while I spent the quarters. Jamie would stand and talk with me while I played the slot machines. I told Jamie that I thought "The Strip" in Vegas was different from "The Strip" in Biloxi, but Jamie didn't want to talk about

"Strips." He liked to talk about cars. He told me that he had always admired the Mustang.

I would look over and see Billy Joe sitting at the tables, and I could see that he was keeping an eye on me. He was among people he knew—the ones he didn't bother to introduce. Some of them had wives or ostentatiously dressed girlfriends with them. They looked like prostitutes to me. Billy Joe didn't like the idea of my sitting at the blackjack tables. He had said "It's no place for you, Baby."

I told Jamie that I had never played slot machines before, but that Billy Joe had taught me to shuffle cards and play poker. I said, "Billy Joe told me I was pretty good one night when Harry was there and we were playing poker while they waited for a phone call. I told Billy Joe I was glad he had taught me to shuffle and play poker. Harry spoke up and said, 'He taught you to shuffle and play—now if he could teach you to win a few, we could take you with us. A poker face like yours could make us some money.'"

Jamie was laughing so hard that Billy Joe left the blackjack table and came over to see what was so funny. Jamie told him that he had never noticed that I had a poker face. Billy Joe said, "But she likes you, Jamie. You should see her around Harry." Jamie started laughing again.

Finally, Billy Joe and I left Caesar's Palace and went to the Sands where he had reservations to see Frank Sinatra. Listening to him sing *Strangers in the Night* on the record at home was nothing like hearing him in person. We had seen Frank Sintra, Jr. at the Domino Lounge in Atlanta, but the Frank Sr. show was awesome. I had worn the same red dress I had on the night we saw Fats Domino in New Orleans. We had always done something special when I wore that red dress.

It was late when the show was over, but we went on to the Sahara and I played the slot machines there. Pretty soon, I ran out of quarters, so we took a cab back to the Casino at the Hilton where I won several times to the tune of about $100.00. I was thrilled; it was the first time I had won anything!

In the elevator on the way to the room, I said, "Billy Joe, I heard a man at Caesar's Palace say that it looked like a Dixie Mafia convention."

Billy Joe let his breath out slowly as he looked toward the ceiling of the elevator and said, "Baby, there's no such thing as the Dixie Mafia, so don't say that word."

"Billy Joe, if there's no such thing, then why do other people say the word?" I asked. He didn't answer. I was still wondering about those people that he didn't introduce to me.

Billy Joe and I spent the day together on Sunday, driving around in his car. I was thinking it was a good thing Billy Joe had driven his car to Vegas instead of Big Red's convertible; the wind in Vegas was blowing as hard as it did on Peachtree at Carnegie Way.

We didn't run into his friends again, and I felt more comfortable when it was just the two of us.

We were riding around and looking at all the sights in Vegas, including the people on the streets. We stopped at a traffic light, and a tall blonde wearing a low-necked blouse that showed a lot of cleavage crossed the street. I told Billy Joe that she was not the first one I had seen with a lot of cleavage in Vegas.

I was reminded of the last reception Sally and I attended after work one Friday. Sally worked for a nice politician from DeKalb County. She and I were both members of the Young Republicans.

I told Billy Joe that Sally and I went to the restroom down the hall from the reception where two secretaries were touching up their makeup at the mirror. The blonde had on a black dress that showed cleavage. She was telling the brunette that she needed to get another dress for these occasions because her boss always wanted her to wear the one that showed a lot of cleavage, and she couldn't keep wearing the same dress.

They went on back to the party. After the door closed behind them, Sally looked in the mirror and said, "I'm glad my boss didn't hire me for my cleavage."

I said, "Me, too. I know why Mr. Green hired me. I heard him telling someone on the phone one day that I could type 132 words a minute and that he didn't worry about how fast my shorthand was because I had a photographic memory."

We rode for a couple of blocks, then I said, "I guess it's a good thing I can type, don't you, Billy Joe? If I don't have cleavage by now, I don't think I'll ever have it, unless I get a boob job."

Billy Joe laughed and said, "Baby, you need a boob job about like you need that piano." I couldn't understand how he compared the two, but that was Billy Joe. I didn't always understand what he meant.

On the way to the airport, Billy Joe asked me if I realized how much money I had lost the night before. I said, "I didn't lose anything. I won about $100.00." He threw his head back and laughed. Then he said that I had not lost as much as he thought I would. As far as I was concerned I had won $100.00. Billy Joe had given me the money to play, but he didn't take my winnings. I couldn't see what difference it made how much of his money I had lost. He had a big wad of money left over after he paid for the room.

During the flight back to Atlanta, I compared our Vegas trip to the New Orleans trip. It was just the two of us in New Orleans. His friends were nowhere around, and Billy Joe was relaxed. I couldn't understand why he acted uneasy when his friends were around—in Atlanta, and in Vegas at Caesar's Palace. I was glad we had not stayed at the same hotel they did. Billy Joe said it was best we didn't.

I wanted to like Billy Joe's friends; he liked all of mine that he had met. He had known Blanche for several years because she worked as a part-time barmaid, but I didn't realize he would know Al.

One day at lunch, I took Billy Joe down to meet Al. They shook hands and Al said, "We've met before, Janie. How are things, Billy Joe?" They talked for a while, and I asked how they knew each other.

Al said, "We've done some business before." I didn't know what business he meant, since Billy Joe didn't need to have things printed.

Then I thought about those raunchy magazines that I ran across one day. When Al noticed I had opened that drawer, he came over and took all the magazines out and placed them in one of those little boxes. He said, "I don't want to have to lock things up around here. You know better than to look at things you're not supposed to look at."

I had never been curious about the contents of those little boxes. Receiving and shipping was a big part of Al's business. He received shipments of big cases, and in each case there were lots of little boxes. People would come down, take little boxes and give Al cash.

Now I wondered if those magazines had anything to do with Billy Joe and his friends. How else would they be doing business? I couldn't think of a single thing that Billy Joe would need to have printed.

I knew there was a pornography king living in Atlanta, and Billy Joe was an acquaintance of his. Billy Joe had driven me by his house one day and had shown me the stone wall that surrounded the house. He told me that Gerald Simpson, a person we both knew from Overton, had erected the wall. I couldn't fathom Gerald attending a small Baptist Church in Overton and building a wall for a porno king.

It was a long and tiring flight, and I was happy to land in Atlanta. I had thought Vegas would be an exciting trip, but it was not as much fun as I thought it would be. The fact that Billy Joe's friends were there spoiled the earlier part of the previous night for me—and for Billy Joe. We would have had more fun if they had been in another state. Billy Joe and I always had more fun when it was just the two of us acting like kids again.

16.

Little Rock to Memphis

Early Sunday morning, I called for a cab to take me to the airport.

Billy Joe had phoned the night before and asked if I would fly down to Jackson and drive home with him. He was waiting at the gate and acted pleased to see me. After he hugged me and relieved me of my tote bag, we headed for the car.

He smiled and shook his head as he placed the tote bag in the trunk. Billy Joe couldn't believe all the things I would carry around in that bag. He had taught me to roll a silk blouse and pants and place them in a shoebox. The shoebox would fit in the bottom of the bag. He said that would keep my clothes free of wrinkles.

I carried the tote bag even when we weren't spending the night. I never knew when I could be stuck somewhere waiting for him. I would take books, sewing, knitting, and whatever else I could think of. This trip was no different.

Billy Joe pulled into the parking lot of a local restaurant for breakfast. It was bone-chilling cold outside and we practically ran from the parking lot to the entrance. I was thinking it was a good thing I had on my long black cashmere coat that I had found on sale at Robert Hall in West End. It was three years old, but it would keep me warm.

When the waitress asked if we would like ham, bacon, or sausage, she reminded me of the waitress at the Pancake House on Peachtree asking Big Red the same question. Big Red had replied, "Yes, please."

The waitress had looked at him and asked, "Which one, sir?"

Big Red had answered, "All of them." He was a big man with a tremendous appetite. However, Big Red wasn't present, so Billy Joe and I ordered bacon.

After breakfast, we faced the bitter cold and made a dash for the car. The weather forecast did not sound good, and I was thankful Billy Joe was driving.

He told me that while we were in Jackson, we would stop by to visit a friend of his. Her name was Rose, and she was the ex-wife of Matthew, the former politician whom I had met in Augusta.

In a few minutes, we were driving down a street with nice, but small, homes. Upon closer observation, I realized they were older, expensive bungalows. Rose's house was painted white and trimmed in dark gray. Billy Joe rang the doorbell. Rose opened the door with a big smile on her face, hugged Billy Joe and said, "So this is Jane. It is such a pleasure to have you here," and she hugged me, too.

Rose was in her early forties, but she looked real good for her age. She wore beige silk pants with a beige print blouse. I wanted an outfit like that.

We sipped tea from fine bone china cups as Rose and Billy Joe chatted about people they both knew. She talked about how difficult it had been for her to accept Matthew's involvement in a fraud scheme. She said she couldn't believe he was sent to prison for signing a few papers. Billy Joe told her that a simple "yes" or "no" was very damaging to someone in Matthew's position. He said that Matthew's signature was all it took for him to be considered guilty.

Rose told us how hurt she had been when their marriage didn't work out after his release. She still couldn't believe he had married Sherry so soon after their divorce.

Then Rose said, "I found out one thing about life—it does go on, whether you want it to or not."

As we finished our tea, Billy Joe told Rose we had better hit the road because the weather was not in his favor that weekend. Rose asked, "How long will it take you to get home?"

Billy Joe replied, "I'm not sure in this weather. Earlier this morning, I found out I would have to be in Memphis tomorrow morning. But first, I have to make a stop in Little Rock. Jane has to work tomorrow, and she can take a flight from Memphis to Atlanta. She's a night owl, so she can catch forty winks in the car."

I was not surprised to hear that. I had caught forty winks in his car and on a plane several times before. Considering that I usually stayed up late, reading or sewing, it made no difference to me if I lost a little sleep.

As we drove toward Little Rock, I was thinking about the time I met Matthew and Sherry. She was younger than Matthew, and I thought it strange that she was always going to the bus station and catching the next bus home every time she and Matthew had a spat. I couldn't visualize Rose doing that. Rose was such a refined Southern lady—not at all like Sherry. I thought Matthew looked and acted like a successful politician, but Billy Joe said Matthew was unable to run for political office again after serving time in prison, and that was why he was selling stocks and bonds. Rose was certainly more his type than Sherry. I was sorry that Matthew and Rose were divorced.

I had not looked at the time when we left Jackson, but I thought we had been on the road over five hours. We had stopped for hamburgers around two o'clock. Billy Joe would be getting hungry again real soon. It was already dark, and flakes of snow had started falling.

When we got to Little Rock, Billy Joe drove through a residential section and stopped at a large two-story white house. He said, "I'll be right back," as he got out of the car and opened the trunk.

A man came out of the house carrying a large metal box. He and Billy Joe talked for two or three minutes, and then I heard a "clunk" as the metal box was placed in the trunk.

Billy Joe got back in the car, and the man threw up his hand as he went back inside the house.

Billy Joe looked over at me and asked, "Are you getting hungry?"

I nodded, "Uh-huh."

He said, "I'll take you to eat at one of my favorite places."

It was a fine seafood restaurant. It was casual, but expensive. I had lobster—the whole thing. I liked lobster, but I had never had a whole one.

I didn't know what I was supposed to do to get to the lobster meat, but I didn't have to worry about that because Billy Joe knew how to do everything. He taught me to eat lobster. I didn't want to unhinge the back and open the lobster. Billy Joe told me to do it anyway, that I needed to know how, just in case.

After finishing, I said, "I'm going to wash my hands."

Billy Joe said, "Use your finger bowl."

I looked at the finger bowl and thought, "That's not enough water to clean these hands." I didn't move a muscle. I sat and stared at the finger bowl. I had never used one before.

Billy Joe showed me how to squeeze the lemon, dip the tips of my fingers, and pat my fingers on the napkin to dry them. I did it, reluctantly, and then I just sat and looked at him. He grinned and said, "Now you can go wash your hands."

On the way to the restroom, I was thinking about the first time we went to Fan and Bill's. I had eaten upstairs at Caesar's Forum, but until that night, I had never had dinner in the main dining room. Billy Joe was telling me how some people would take the net off the lemon in a fine dining room, then squeeze the lemon and squirt it in somebody's eye.

"Baby, they don't know to leave the net on the lemon. There's a reason for that net being there—so the lemon juice won't squirt in somebody's eye. They're paying for that net, so they need to leave it alone," he said. "It's not like at home where there's just a little saucer of sliced lemon on the table, and people with manners hold one hand over the lemon when they squeeze it."

I understood the real reason he had told me about the net on the lemon. He was afraid I would sit there and take that net off the lemon in front of the customers and those waiters who were standing by looking straight ahead but seeing every move I made. I didn't know why I was so intimidated by waiters. Maybe it was because they certainly understood more about fine dining than I did, and I knew they made more money than I did. I wished I could just stick to eating in places where the waiters and waitresses acted like real people, and I could even make conversation with them if I wanted to. Billy Joe told me not to make conversation with waiters in fine dining places. He said it wasn't necessary.

I remembered the first time we were served sorbet. I thought it was too early for dessert, but Billy Joe told me it wasn't dessert. He said, "Sorbet is served between courses to cleanse the palate so that you can taste the true flavor of each course."

I asked Billy Joe how he knew all about fine dining and he said, "Baby, I paid for lessons on fine dining when I found out that Aunt Aggie's 'mind your manners' program just didn't work—out here in the real world."

We had finished eating and were headed to the car when Billy Joe said, "You can drive from here." He ushered me to the driver's door, opened it, and stood there while I got in.

I didn't want to drive. My black cashmere coat had turned white just running to the car. The snow was wet, but it was sticking. My coat would be ruined. The wind was blowing and my hair was a mess. Billy Joe went around and got in the car. He said, "It's slippery out there, Baby, so be careful."

"Be careful? Billy Joe, I can't believe you're making me drive through this! Don't you remember that day we were at Aunt Aggie's and I had to go down to the funeral home and pay my respects because Mrs. Blevins, who used to be my neighbor, died? You didn't even want me to drive your car that short distance. You said, 'What if you have a wreck? There's ice on the road.' I told you I had to go and that I could drive on the ice. You told me to go on, but to be careful.

"There was no one in the Blevins family there, so I stayed only five minutes. And I brought your car back in one piece, didn't I? Now you want me to drive through this blizzard, and you don't seem one bit worried!"

I remembered that I parked around back at the funeral home. Carlton, the owner of the funeral home, met me at the back door. He looked at me, looked out at the car, and said, "Whose car are you in?" I didn't even answer him. He asked, "Is it Billy Joe's?" Then he grinned. I wondered how he recognized Billy Joe's car. I didn't know of any occasion that he would have had to meet Billy Joe or recognize his car since he was not even living in Overton when Billy Joe was in school. I just walked on past him and stopped to sign the guest book located near the front entrance.

I didn't tell Billy Joe that Milton Riggs was at the funeral home that day. Milton was the deputy sheriff, and he was a friend of Daddy's. I had just signed the guest book when Milton came up to me and asked, in his deep Southern drawl, "How are you doing, Jane?"

I looked at him, smiled and said, "Fine, how are you?"

Milton stood there for what seemed like a long time, then he said, "I need to talk to you." He motioned toward the corner of the room near the fireplace and followed me there.

He looked me square in the eye and said, "Jane, you're over twenty-one now, and I want you to know that you need to watch what you're doing and watch the company you're keeping. If you get into anything away from Overton, there's not a damn thing I can do to help you. I want you to think about that." Then he turned and walked out.

I waited until his car was gone from the parking lot, then I left the funeral home, too. Well, I didn't see any need to bring that up now. I had to concentrate on driving.

The snow looked like a fine mist, but it was thick, and the wind was howling. I had been driving about thirty minutes when Billy Joe said,

"Watch it. There's a truck ahead. Don't pass it; just stay a good distance behind it so you can see the lights."

I said, "Billy Joe, I'm not gonna pass anything on this road! Don't you understand that I don't want to drive this car, and I don't want to go to Memphis! Why didn't you put me on a plane in Little Rock? You know I have to be at work in the morning."

Billy Joe just sat there, staring ahead. Then, in his most serious voice, he said, "Baby, I have to be in Memphis in the morning. That's just as important to me as your getting to work on time is to you. I don't fly in planes, and I don't drive in blizzards. You're my only chance to get there. Can't you bear with me this once?"

I thought about what he said. Billy Joe rarely asked me to do anything for him. I guessed it was the least I could do. And I was a good driver.

I had stopped gripping the steering wheel and had relaxed somewhat when I saw a dim light in the rearview mirror. I said, "Billy Joe, it's not just us and that truck ahead now; here comes another car. I can see a dim light behind us." Then I could hear the noise. It was another truck.

Billy Joe said, "Hold it steady on the road. That truck could vibrate the car a little bit, but don't panic." The truck was real loud as it approached. It sounded like thunder. Then it went on by.

Billy Joe said, "I'm glad it's ahead of us and not behind us. Keep following the first truck."

I was feeling a little better about driving. I was scared when I first got on the freeway, but it was easier following the dim light on the truck ahead. I hoped he wouldn't speed up, because I didn't think I could drive any faster. I felt so much better, I turned to Billy Joe and said, "Billy Joe, isn't there a song, something about 40 miles of bad road?"

Billy Joe said, "Watch the road. Yes, but you've got almost 140 miles to Memphis."

Billy Joe turned on the radio. I said, "Billy Joe, please don't have the radio on."

"Why not?" he asked. "You always like music."

"I know it, Billy Joe, but I can't see with the radio on," I said.

"What has the radio got to do with your seeing?" he asked.

I thought about it for a minute and then I replied, "Well, maybe I can still see, but I guess what I'm trying to say is that I can't *think* with the radio on."

Billy Joe laughed, turned off the radio, and said, "You don't have to think. Just follow that truck."

The snow was still coming down, but it was not as thick. We had been on the road for over four hours, and I was happy to be seeing outlines of something other than just the dim tail lights of the truck ahead. It was a good thing I had gone to the restroom in Little Rock.

There was an all-night diner ahead. The truck pulled off there. So did I.

We were sitting in a booth having coffee and waiting for our food. Billy Joe lit a cigarette and handed it to me. He said, "If you can go four hours, you don't have to smoke at all. I'm proud of you, Baby."

My mouth was wide open. I said, "Billy Joe, you would pitch a fit if I lit a cigarette in your car and didn't crack the window—and the weather was too bad."

He looked straight at me and asked, "Have you ever seen me pitch a fit?"

"No," I replied.

The waitress placed our food on the table. When she moved away from the table, Billy Joe asked, "Have I ever asked you to crack a window?"

Looking down at my plate, I said, "No, but I thought…"

I looked up. Billy Joe was already eating and pretending he was not paying one bit of attention to what I was saying. It was obvious when he was pretending to ignore me. And I also knew he pretended to pay no attention when he wanted me to be quiet. I could have gotten into a number of arguments with him, but he just wasn't the arguing type. I was miffed! I could have been smoking the whole trip!

The only reason I thought I had to crack a window was because I saw him do it. And he had told me one time that the reason he held his cigarette away from the windshield was because he didn't want the smoke to make a film on the windshield. I held mine away from the windshield, too. I could take a hint.

We finished eating, and Billy Joe walked up to the cash register and got change from the cashier. Then he used the pay phone.

When he came back to the booth, he said, "Baby, there's a flight to Atlanta at 5:00 A.M. You're booked on it. That gives you enough time to fly, take a cab home, get dressed and get to work on time. I knew you would get us here. If I mention getting to work on time, you can drive through hell and high water."

Billy Joe acted so happy that I thought it was worth all the initial horror I had been through to get us to Memphis. Maggie had told me that I was a good driver; and Lucky had always said that I was a survivor. They were right!

17.

Dixie Mafia

I was in the office early on Tuesday morning. Mr. Green was already there, but he had to leave for the airport. Al called at 11:30 and asked if I could do some invoicing on my lunch hour. I ran over to the deli earlier than usual to beat the lunch crowd, ordered a chopped liver on onion roll to go, and dashed down the street to Al's shop.

As I ate lunch and typed invoices, Al turned on the 12:00 news. They were bringing an update on a burglary that had happened Sunday night. It seemed that two men had gone into a nearby appliance store through the roof and cracked the safe. There was evidence of dirt and dust tracked from the ducts to the safe.

They got away, but there was a witness who saw two men getting into a black Mustang around eleven o'clock on Sunday night. The witness said that one of the men was short with dark hair and looked real dirty and smudged.

I said to Al, "They must have been pretty stupid, burglarizing a place on such a clear night. It's no wonder somebody saw them."

Al asked, "Why do you say that?"

"One rainy night when we were riding down Peachtree, Billy Joe said, 'The burglars are out tonight.' I asked him what he meant and he told me that when the weather was rainy, foggy, or cold and windy, the burglars were out because people were not paying attention to them. He said most people were trying to get inside, out of the weather."

In a sarcastic voice, Al asked, "Are Billy Joe's buddies in town this week?"

I said, "Yes, and I know what you're thinking, Al, but Billy Joe and his friends would never do anything like that. He told me he had taken a safe only once in his life and that was when he was in high school. He and two of his friends took the safe from the school office out into the woods behind the school. Mr. Sanders called them into the office, made them go get it, and made them promise never to take a safe again. Billy Joe said that he promised. They didn't even call the police. Said it was just a teenage prank."

Al grunted and said, "They got into a black Mustang."

"I know it, Al, but I know where my car was. Billy Joe took it when he left at 10:30 Sunday night so he could have the oil changed on Monday. He had it washed and waxed, too."

Al said, "To remove fingerprints? Jane, you need to be very careful. I would hate to see you come to a rude awakening."

"Al, don't say that," I replied. "My daddy has always said to me, 'Young lady, one day you'll come to a rude awakening.' I can't stand those words."

Al snorted a lot and finally he said, "I have to tell you something and it's difficult for me. You won't listen to your own daddy, so I guess it's my job to say it. You need to do something about Billy Joe. You're a smart kid, and you don't need him."

I said, "Yes, I do. And he needs me, too. One time he said if it were not for me, he could just go crawl in a hole somewhere."

Al said, "That wouldn't be a bad idea, so long as he didn't take you with him."

"Why do you say that, Al? Don't you like Billy Joe?"

"Yes, Janie, I like Billy Joe. Everybody likes Billy Joe. I hate to be the one to break the news to you, but Billy Joe is not what you think he is. I don't think he has robbed any banks or killed anyone, but you need to get away from those people. He's a good boy, but he's running with a bunch of thugs called the Dixie Mafia," said Al.

"That's not true, Al. I know because I asked Billy Joe one night when Harry came by to pick him up. They were looking at the news and

Harry said, 'Wait and see. They'll blame that one on the Dixie Mafia. Yeah, boy. Every time some punk goes out and does something stupid, they call it the Dixie Mafia. That really burns me up.'

"I was at the table sewing, but my ears perked up. I looked at them and asked, 'What is the Dixie Mafia?' Billy Joe told me there was no such thing as the Dixie Mafia, and that someone just made up that name to sell more newspapers in Biloxi."

Al said, "See—Biloxi. So there you go. Don't you know that Billy Joe stays in Biloxi when he's not here?"

"I know it, Al," I said, "but he has nice friends down there. I've met them." Al made a strange noise that sounded like a snort again, and walked over to the files. I kept doing the invoicing.

The next morning, Al called me at work. He said, "Your boyfriend is in jail. His name is in the paper. There was a burglary at an exclusive dress shop a few weeks ago. If he has given you any clothes in the past several weeks, go home and get them. Bring them down here."

I went into a zombie state. I told him Billy Joe gave me three dresses that Renee didn't like because they were too plain for her. He said, "Go get them now. It's almost time for your lunch anyway."

I didn't falter. Hopping on a bus in front of the building, I went home and placed the dresses in a Franklin Simon shopping bag. Boarding a southbound bus, shopping bag in hand, I headed for the print shop. Al placed the bag in a big dusty box, sealed it, and put it on the top shelf with all those other grimy boxes. We made no conversation.

The trip had taken all of fifteen minutes. I grabbed a sandwich at the deli and carried it back to the office. There were two men leaning against the wall at the elevator when I got off on my floor. Their eyebrows shot up as soon as they saw me stepping off the elevator. With a look of bewilderment, one of them asked, "Early lunch?"

I replied, "I'm hungry." The truth was that I didn't think I could ever swallow again. At five o'clock, I threw the sandwich in the trash and left the office.

I felt so nervous, so confused, and so scared, that I was still acting like a robot when I arrived home from work. The phone was ringing. I answered, and it was Renee. She said, "I wanted to call you at work, but I didn't know the number. What did you do with those clothes I sent you?"

I told her I had gotten rid of them on my lunch hour. She said, "We appreciate that. Obviously you're not as dumb as you act. But I don't think it's right that you get all the benefits and never get your hands dirty."

I asked her what benefits. She said, "That nice apartment and everything else Billy Joe does for you."

I told her I paid my own rent. The only thing I could think of was the money I had left over from the cab fares. But that was none of her business, so I didn't mention it.

I said, "Billy Joe told me I made as much as a cheap divorce lawyer working as hard as I do. And he told me a long time ago that he didn't want to get involved in my finances, because if anything ever happened to him, he didn't want to leave me in a bind."

She said, "Well, the ironic thing is that something has happened to him, and he's in jail for something he didn't do. He was with you that night of the burglary. The two of you were down at his Aunt Aggie's, eating homemade chicken pot pie. You're his only alibi, but he won't let his lawyer use you. So he's going to stay in jail, all because of you. I just don't understand it. You're such an encumbrance to him, and he still wants to see you Saturday. He said for you to tell them you're his sister. Your name is on the list to see him."

"Renee, if he didn't do anything wrong, why is he in jail?" I asked.

She answered, "Harry and I were staying at the Riviera, and Billy Joe came by to have lunch with us. We were ready to walk out the door when there was a knock. Harry opened the door, and there stood two detectives with a search warrant. Some of the clothes that were taken in the burglary were in the room. So they took all of us in, but my lawyer called a few people and I was released. Billy Joe just happened to be there at the wrong time."

I said, "Well, tell him I'll be there Saturday."

As soon as I hung up the phone, I called Phoebe and said, "You won't believe this. Remember the last time we were down at Mona's getting our fortunes read? She told me that she could see two men, a woman, a knock at the door, and two policemen. Well, it happened! Not to me, but to Billy Joe." Then I told Phoebe what Renee had said.

Phoebe said, "You know that Mona has been accurate in her predictions before. Now I don't know what to think. I believe she really can see the future in those cards."

"Well, Phoebe, it scares me to death. I don't think I'll ever go back there. I don't want to know what's in the cards for me."

We talked about how strange Mona's prediction was and then we hung up the phone. It was difficult for me to go to sleep that night.

I made it through the week, and on Saturday morning, I headed out to visit Billy Joe. I had never been to a jail before. I dreaded seeing Billy Joe, but I understood I had to do it. I went through a long line of visitors and followed the same procedures as they did. When asked the relationship, I answered "sister." I was superstitious, so my fingers were crossed when I said it.

When I finally reached the end of the visitor's line, I followed one of the men in uniform up several steps. Then he led me through the two sets of double doors that made a loud clank when they closed. I went into a small room and there sat Billy Joe behind the window. He was the only one in the room.

I sat down in a chair in front of the window. Billy Joe didn't look happy to see me. I said, "Billy Joe, if you were with me, why don't you tell them?"

He stared ahead and said, "I can't, Baby. I've been in jail before, but you've never been cross-examined. I just can't let that happen." We sat in silence.

18.

The Big Diamond

Renee called on Wednesday night and told me that Billy Joe would be released from jail on Saturday and that he would like to see me Saturday evening around six o'clock.

She said, "Harry and I want to thank you for standing by him. Most people like you would have run the other way when he went to jail."

I answered, "Thank goodness he's getting out. Tell him I'll be here Saturday."

There was no need for her to thank me. Renee acted like she and Harry were family, and I resented that.

Billy Joe called at five o'clock on Saturday afternoon. He said, "I'll be there in an hour, Baby. Sorry I missed your birthday. I'm bringing your birthday present and we'll go to dinner. Is that okay with you?"

I replied, "I'm happy to hear from you, Billy Joe. And yes, I would like that very much." I was so excited, I didn't know what to do. But I would not dare let Billy Joe know how excited I was to hear from him and how glad I was that he was out of jail. He would shrug off that much attention.

He had said he was sorry he missed my birthday, but he didn't miss it. He ignored it. I would never forget! The only birthday in my life that had not been celebrated was on the day that I visited Billy Joe in jail. I didn't even remember my own birthday that year.

At six o'clock, the doorbell rang. There was Billy Joe, standing at the door with a big smile on his face and a gift-wrapped box in his arms. He walked in and set the box on the table. Then he hugged me and said, "Happy Birthday, Baby. I want you to open your present now."

He handed me the big square box that was wrapped in blue and white with a big blue ribbon. I carefully removed the paper and ribbon and found that the square box contained four smaller boxes of shoes—Ferragamo and I. Miller heels. I had never had shoes that dainty and expensive, and four pairs in one day were beyond my imagination.

Billy Joe said, "The receipt is in one of the boxes, so that if they don't fit, or if you don't like them, we can make a trip to Neiman Marcus in Dallas and get what you like. I've heard they're planning to build in Atlanta, but that's gonna take a while."

I said, "This is overwhelming, Billy Joe. What made you buy so many shoes?"

With an earnest look on his face, he replied, "Every time I see a shoe store, I think of you. I know you have a closet full now, but I also know you can always use more. In fact, I started to give you these shoes a long time before your birthday. Now I wish I had. They've been down at Aunt Aggie's since the last time I was in Dallas. I showed them to Aunt Aggie. She said they were real pretty and she thought they would look good on you."

Then he asked if I was ready to go to dinner.

I wanted to wear a pair of the new shoes, but considering the outfit I was wearing, I thought those shoes were too dressy. I would have to wait to wear them.

We ate at Seven Steers in Buckhead where Blanche was serving drinks in the bar. She acted happy to see us, but I could see the arch of her right eyebrow. It still reminded me of a question mark. I could tell that she was thinking about the night at Mama Mia's restaurant, and so was I. But it was obvious that everything was definitely all right between Billy Joe and me. I had talked with her several times since moving downtown and had visited her twice, so she was aware that I didn't see Billy Joe every night. She also realized he was out of town a lot.

Billy Joe didn't seem to be hungry during dinner. He said he wished he had some of Aunt Aggie's homemade chicken pot pie. "I don't know how you eat those frozen ones from the store, Baby. That's all you've got in the freezer. How do you stand to eat them, after sampling Aunt Aggie's with real ingredients? She uses chopped boiled eggs, English peas, carrots, and chicken broth that she thickens. I don't know what all she puts in it, but it's my favorite meal," said Billy Joe.

He was probably thinking of being in jail and his only alibi had been that we were together at Aunt Aggie's. But he would never allow either of us to go to court, and he had not mentioned being in jail. Then, suddenly, that little grin appeared on his face.

He said, "Baby, you're not gonna believe this. I still don't believe it myself, but thanks to your daddy's friend, Milton Riggs, I'm out of jail. I'll bet ol' Milton doesn't believe it either."

"What are you talking about, Billy Joe?" I asked.

"Do you remember the afternoon we went down to Aunt Aggie's? The same day you drove my car to the funeral home, and when you came back we had chicken pot pie? Then the ice and snow got worse, so we spent the night there?"

I said, "Yes, but what's that got to do with Milton Riggs?"

Billy Joe replied, "My attorney asked me if there could be anyone else in the whole world who knew for a fact that I spent that night at Aunt Aggie's. He asked if there was anyone else who saw me. That's when I remembered the black woman with a white rag on her head, beating on the door after midnight. I heard her hollering, 'Help me. They're after me.'"

"The only thing I remember, Billy Joe, is that when Aunt Aggie and I jumped out of bed to see what was going on, you were already in the living room. You made us go back to bed. You said, 'Get away from the windows and door. Go back to bed. Somebody could be shooting at her.' We went back to the bedroom, and you called the sheriff's office."

"That's right, Baby. And Milton Riggs was on duty that night. When he drove up, the woman was lying down in Aunt Aggie's boxwoods near the front door. He thanked me for calling, and he told me that the woman was sick and had these fits sometimes. He said he would take her home. It was almost one o'clock in the morning."

"Will Milton tell them he saw you, Billy Joe?" I asked.

"They keep good records in Overton, Baby. It's all there, the date and time, in black-and-white. Harry bonded out of jail, too, but he has to go to court. I told Harry that the next time I went to Overton for chicken pot pie, he would be wise to go with me. That's why I've declared chicken pot pie as my favorite meal."

Then Billy Joe acted famished. He ate everything on his plate.

After dinner, we browsed around in a few shops. In one of the jewelry stores, we looked at pendants and bracelets.

I was still looking at a counter of bracelets when Billy Joe took my arm and said, "Let's go."

He literally pushed me out the door and practically ran to the car, holding my hand all the while. He opened my door and said, "Move, move." I could always tell something was wrong when he did a double word. He went around to his side of the car, got in, and drove off real fast.

I said, "Billy Joe, what's your hurry?"

He said, "What if I took a diamond at that store? Wouldn't you be in a hurry if you took one?"

I looked at him and said, "Why are you asking me a question like that? You didn't take a diamond."

He replied, "Yes, I did."

Billy Joe had never driven that fast before while I was in the car. I wanted him to slow down, but he kept up the speed. I said, "Don't go so fast, Billy Joe. It scares me. Are you trying to scare me?"

"No, Baby, I'm not trying to do anything except get on the freeway as soon as I can."

When he entered the freeway at Piedmont, I said, "What's wrong? Why are you still driving fast?"

That's when he told me that he had taken a diamond and that he was sorry. He said he didn't mean to, but the opportunity was there, and he had to do it. Then he said, "That's what I do, Baby. I want you to know that I've never harmed a soul, but I have hurt a few insurance companies."

He was making me nervous. I said, "Tell me the truth."

"Baby, you wouldn't know the truth if it hit you in the eye. You see what you want to see, and you believe what you want to believe. But you can believe this—I have never lied to you."

I said, "Let me see it then."

"I can't; it's in my mouth," he said. "If I'm stopped, I can swallow it. Then I won't be caught red-handed."

I thought to myself that he wouldn't be swallowing a diamond. It would probably kill him. That's when I said, "Don't be ridiculous. People don't swallow diamonds." I thought it was impossible.

It didn't take us long to get home. When we were inside the apartment, I said, "I don't believe you. You were just trying to scare me. If you really did, let me see it."

"No, I can't. If you see it, that would make you an accessory after the fact. That is, unless you turned me in. And I'd like to think you wouldn't do that. If you don't see it, then you can't say I took it. I've got to go. I'll give you a call later," he said.

I stood in the foyer a long time before I could even move. I was wondering if he really took a diamond, and then I thought it was impossible. It was inconceivable to me that he would ever do anything like that!

On Monday, I was surprised to receive a dozen red roses at the office. The card was signed, "Love."

He called two days later and said, "Miss Moss? This is Billy Joe." He was throwing the hat in first—again.

Since I pretended to myself that the diamond episode had never happened, I saw him that evening for dinner. After dinner, we browsed through Rich's downtown store.

The coat was suede with a mink collar. It was on a mannequin. Billy Joe asked me if I liked the coat, and we stood and looked at it. Then we moved on. When we came back by, I noticed that the mannequin was nude. I said, "What happened to that coat, Billy Joe? Do you think someone bought it?"

Billy Joe kept walking. He turned to me and said, "I thought you said you liked it, so I got it for you."

"Well, where is it then?"

He kept smiling. "I have it. Don't worry."

"Not again," I replied. "I will not leave this store until you put it back where you got it. They won't arrest you until you leave, and if you leave, it will be without me."

"Ah, Baby, don't make me do that."

I turned and walked back to the mannequin. I wouldn't budge an inch until he put it back. While he was re-dressing the mannequin, the sales lady came up. She acted nervous and asked, "Could I help you, Sir?"

By then, Billy Joe was buttoning the coat. He said, "I thought she wanted the coat, but then she said she didn't, so I'm putting it back where I got it. Is that okay with you?"

The lady was fidgety and started looking around for her supervisor or security. Billy Joe slowly finished buttoning the coat, turned to the lady and said, "Maybe next time."

As we left the store, I said, "Billy Joe, one day there will be a law against intimidating sales people. Just you wait and see."

He replied, "Ah, step it."

Then we dropped in one of the dime stores down the street. I think it was a Woolworth's.

Billy Joe said he wanted to buy me a peace offering for scaring me. So he did. It was an antique-colored coin bracelet and the price was only $2.98.

After he paid for it, he stood at the cash register, opened it, and placed it on my arm. He leaned down and kissed me on the cheek as the cashier and all the people behind us looked on. They cheered. I was not even embarrassed.

Then he laughed and said, "I would like to give you a diamond, but people might think it was stolen."

Later, I found out they would have. But I wore that bracelet, and I loved that bracelet. It meant more to me than any diamond ever could.

19.

Church

On a cold and rainy Sunday morning, I was listening to church music on the radio and sewing. When I was a teenager, my grandmother, Mimi, would say, "Sunday is the Sabbath and you don't need to be sewing or working on Sunday. Remember 'Six days thou shalt work and on the seventh, thou shalt rest.'"

I asked, "Then why do you hem things on Sunday, Mimi?" She told me there were times when the "ox got in the ditch" and she had to do it. Mimi was always quoting from the scriptures and *Good Housekeeping* magazine. Sometimes I couldn't tell which; I thought it was possibly a combination of both.

The music was playing *Peace, Be Still.* I thought of Billy Joe. I knew the "tempests were raging" in him. Or something was. He just couldn't be still anymore. I sat and looked out the window at the thick mist falling from the sky. That mist reminded me of our trip to Helen, Georgia.

Billy Joe had called on a Sunday morning and said, "Why don't we ride up to Helen?"

My reply had been "Why would you want to go there?" Then I thought, here I go again, answering a question with a question. But Billy Joe didn't seem to notice that time.

He said, "It's October—time for Octoberfest. And we need to go see the leaves change colors."

I told him that there were plenty of leaves in Overton that changed colors every year, and I didn't see any reason to go that far just to see the leaves. He said it would do me good to get out, and he would be by to pick me up in a little while.

When Billy Joe arrived, I was ready to go. He said, "You'd better take a coat. It could get a little chilly." He reached in the closet and removed my red wool coat. We went out to the parking lot. I didn't see his car, but he walked over to a little black sports car and opened the door for me. The car was a convertible with the top down. As I got in, I asked, "Where did you get this car?"

"I borrowed it for the trip. I thought you would enjoy riding in it," he replied. I was glad I had my coat. The sun was shining brightly, but I knew how chilly it would be in the mountains. We talked and laughed all the way to Helen. My hair was a fright, but I didn't care. I could see that Billy Joe was having fun.

We parked the car and walked through several of the shops. There were people partying everywhere. For lunch, we ate Bratwurst sandwiches, potato salad, and had German beer at an outdoor restaurant overlooking the Chattahoochee River. My first beer, and I thought the taste was repulsive. For dessert, Billy Joe suggested the Apple Strudel, served hot with whipped cream.

After lunch, we sat and drank coffee as we listened to the rush of the Chattahoochee and the live music. They were playing *Beer Barrel Polka*.

The temperature was definitely dropping, and Billy Joe said it would be a good idea to get on back to Atlanta, since he didn't have the top for the car. He explained that in such a small car, the top was removed, so there was not one to "let up" on the way home.

I was huddled underneath my coat in the car. Billy Joe was singing, "Roll out the barrel, we'll have a barrel of fun. Roll out the barrel, we've got the blues on the run."

We were halfway home when I raised my head and felt something wet. I said, "Billy Joe, it's raining."

Billy Joe glanced over at me, and in a monotone, he said, "It's not raining, Baby."

I said, "Well, if it's not raining, why do you have the wipers on?"

In another monotone, he said, "To keep the sleet from accumulating on the windshield."

"Sleet?" I raised my head all the way up. Sleet was hitting me in the face. I covered my head completely. I didn't want to think about riding in the sleet. Billy Joe and I didn't exchange another word all the way home.

I knew we were in the parking lot when Billy Joe backed the car into the space. I raised my head again. The interior of the car was wet. I felt like a drowned rat would feel. I was sure of it. We rushed from the parking lot through the tunnel to the building. When we walked through the door to the apartment, Billy Joe said, "Go take a hot shower so you won't be sick."

As it turned out, Billy Joe was the one who got sick. He was there for three days, too sick to leave. I came home every day at lunch to check on him. He was having chills and fever. Fortunately, he had laundry and dry cleaning there that I had picked up for him at Mac and Jac's the previous week.

He told me that he had called Tony to come pick up the car. He said Tony stopped by and got the keys, and in a few minutes, he was back to get a towel. Tony told Billy Joe that even though it was parked on the fourth floor of the covered parking deck, the car was still damp. The seats were leather, but the carpeting was plush and had made a "squish" noise when he stepped inside.

On the third night, Billy Joe was feeling better. I said to him, "The interior of that car was probably ruined. Who does that car belong to anyway?" I didn't think it was Tony's.

He said, "Some prostitute. I borrowed it from Tony."

I said, "I can't believe I've been all the way to Helen, Georgia, and back, in a prostitute's car, and almost drowned in the process. And then you got sick and I thought you were going to die in my bed. How could I ever explain your being here? Why do you put me through things like this, Billy Joe?"

Billy Joe grinned and said, "I wanted you to have fun. And if I had died, you could have just thrown me down that garbage chute of yours."

I had to laugh.

Then the doorbell interrupted my thoughts. It was Billy Joe. He had called earlier and asked if he could bring my breakfast. I told him he could. I never ate breakfast except with Billy Joe. He said breakfast was the most important meal of the day. He also told me that since I didn't usually eat breakfast, I should add sugar to my coffee if I wanted my brain to work. I thought my brain worked fine, but some days, when Mr. Green was in the office, I would add sugar to my coffee.

Billy Joe brought the food in and removed plates from the cabinet. He never ate out of a "to-go" box. He always used a plate, and he would set the table, using cloth napkins. Billy Joe had class, and he made me feel special.

While we were eating, the church music was still playing on the radio. Billy Joe said the music reminded him of what he needed to tell me. And then he went into his little speech—again—about how it wasn't a good idea for him to keep seeing me. He told me that I should find a good man who went to church, marry him, and live happily ever after.

I just listened. I knew he would never stop seeing me.

I said, "Well, you could go to church with me, Billy Joe. We could even go to a Catholic Church. I have friends who do, and they go confess their sins and get forgiveness. We could do that."

Billy Joe laughed and said, "I can't think of any sins that you need to confess, unless it's spending too much money on shoes. Ever since you hemmed Mia's skirt and saw the floor of her closet covered in tissue paper and all those expensive no-scuff-marked shoes lined up, you haven't been the same. For goodness sakes, Baby, Mia is a model with J. P. Allen. They furnish her shoes."

"I have more sins than you know, Billy Joe. Do you remember telling me that you couldn't cheat an honest man? Well, you can cheat an honest company. Mr. Green does. That's how he got that color TV for the office," I said.

Billy Joe looked at me real hard and asked, "What do you mean, Baby?" I told him how Mr. Green had a friend who worked at an office supply place, and every time I ordered supplies from them, the friend would place 40% of the cost on a credit for Mr. Green. Then, when there was a substantial amount of money on the credit balance, Mr. Green would buy something with it. "Don't you think that's stealing?" I asked.

Billy Joe said, "Explain how that's stealing. The TV is still in your office."

"I know it, but it's got a sticker on the back that says it is the personal property of Hiram H. Green. That means if he leaves the company, he'll take it with him. And if I know this, does it make me an accessory? You told me one time if I knew something for a fact that I could be an accessory. You said if I didn't know it for a fact that I couldn't be one.

"I know this for a fact. And he goes to church every Sunday. It's not a Catholic Church, but I guess he prays for God to forgive his sins. I don't think he's told God about the TV though, do you? I know that when I pray, I don't have to tell God everything; he already knows," I said.

Billy Joe glanced at me and asked, "What do you pray about?"

I said, "Well, every night, I say the same 'Now I lay me down to sleep' that I've said since I was a child. And at the end I still say, 'God bless Mother, Daddy, Johnny and Donna.' The reason I say to bless Donna is because Mimi told me to. She told me Donna was the baby of the family and that's why she was so spoiled. She said the reason Donna was so spiteful to me was that she wanted all the attention for herself.

"Mimi said I received enough attention from Lucky and everybody else, so not to worry about Donna—that one day Donna and I would be close friends. I can't see that day ever happening.

"And now, I always add, 'And please bless Billy Joe.' I use the word 'please' when you've been gone a long time and you haven't called. Do you ever pray, Billy Joe?"

"Sometimes, Baby, sometimes," he said.

"Well, what do you pray about?" I asked.

"I pray that I won't hurt the people who care about me, and the people I care about," said Billy Joe.

"Do you name every one of them, like I do?" I asked.

"No, Baby. It's just Aunt Aggie, Cheryl, Tammy, and you. It's a short list, and as you said, God already knows the people I care about. I don't need to name them." He got up from the table and started clearing the dishes.

I returned the salt and pepper to the kitchen and asked, "Do you think you will ever be in church again?"

Billy Joe stood at the sink, staring down at the floor. As I turned to leave, I heard him say, "One day."

Billy Joe stayed a little while longer, and after he left, I wondered why he kept bringing up the subject of my marrying a nice man. I could have married a nice man who went to church every Sunday, if it had not been for that beauty contest when I was in the eleventh grade.

It was a countywide contest held at the basketball gym during the county fair. There were not many junior and senior girls watching from the stands in the gym—almost all of us were in the contest. I was standing next to Claire as the winners were being announced. Claire had already taken off her shoes when her name was called as first runner up. Then the queen of the fair was announced. I was not surprised that it turned out to be Glenda Milsaps, a very pretty girl in my class.

I could see "Catfish" sitting in the stands with some of the basketball players. His name was Russ, but my daddy called him "Catfish." Daddy said Russ was "all mouth and no brains."

Russ was a preacher's son. We were a twosome around school and attended basketball games on Tuesday and Friday nights. Russ was a basketball player and I was a cheerleader. We usually saw a movie on Saturday nights, and sometimes we would attend his daddy's church on Sunday nights.

A week or so after the beauty contest, I learned that Russ was seeing Glenda Milsaps. He never said anything to me about it, and we didn't break up. We just drifted apart and remained friends. Later, when a girl in my class asked why I was not dating Russ, I replied, "He's dating a pretty girl now." We laughed about that.

As fate would have it, Russ didn't marry Glenda either. He met a cheerleader at another school and married her. She was even prettier than Glenda, and I was sure they attended church every Sunday.

I was happy with my present fate. If I had married a nice man who went to church every Sunday, I wouldn't be seeing Billy Joe. And I would rather be seeing him.

20.

Merry Christmas

Two weeks before Christmas, Billy Joe and I were sitting in the living room watching television. I was looking at the new green antique satin drapes—an early Christmas present from Billy Joe. He had them custom-made by a friend who owned an interior decorating company. I was happy with the furnished vertical blinds that covered the ten-foot sliding glass door, but Billy Joe said the drapes would add character to the room.

I usually left the drapes open so I could see what was happening on the street. I told Billy Joe that I thought it was getting dangerous to be on the streets around Christmas time and that a man had been mugged in front of my building.

I said, "When Kate and I came home in a cab from the Civic Center one night, a police car was here and a Grady ambulance was taking the man to the hospital. He was wearing a suit and a nice camel overcoat. The hippies are wandering south of Tenth Street into my own neighborhood. They probably mugged that man."

Billy Joe said, "Hippies didn't do that, Baby. Local punks do things like that. Sometimes they dress like hippies, but you can tell by looking at their eyes. Real hippies look straight ahead. If they have shifty eyes, they're not real hippies. And you need to be careful walking through that tunnel from the parking lot between now and Christmas. Why don't you take a cab at night? There should be plenty of money in your cookie jar on the refrigerator."

I didn't know how much money was in the cookie jar, but Billy Joe saw that there was always enough to pay for a cab to the airport and purchase an airline ticket, in case he called me to meet him somewhere. I had always kept that money separate and had put the change back in the cookie jar every time I used some of it. I had never thought about using that money for anything else.

Billy Joe was amused at the way I separated money in several envelopes in my bag. One envelope was marked "extra money." He called that one my "stash." I didn't tell him about my real stash at Atlanta Federal. I had been saving there since I was eighteen years old.

He knew I wouldn't eat at the Crystal, even when we were in a hurry, but he didn't know that the reason dated back to 1961. When I lived with Lucky and Gina, she would take my check every payday and deposit the entire check, except for $10.00 a week, into my savings account at Atlanta Federal where she worked. She would give me the $10.00 for lunch and incidentals. I didn't want to waste money on food, so I ate at the Crystal across from Leb's almost every day at lunch. I was happy that Gina had taught me to save money, but since that time, I had not been able to eat at the Crystal.

I started to tell Billy Joe about the Crystal, but when I looked over at him, I could see that he was getting restless watching television. Finally, he said, "Baby, why don't we go out and get some Christmas spirit?" So we spent all afternoon downtown at Davison's and Rich's, and out at Lenox Mall.

Christmas music was everywhere. We even bought a tree, took it home, and trimmed it. Billy Joe picked out all the ornaments. He had selected wooden hand-painted elves, snowmen, toy soldiers, Santas, angels, train engines, and gingerbread men. There was a small angel on top. The lights were tiny, clear ones. When they blinked, the ornaments would stand out and look real. We had so much fun decorating that tree. I thought it was the most beautiful tree I had ever seen.

While I put away all the boxes and placed the debris in the trash, Billy Joe made hot apple cider. He brought it to the living room and we sat on the sofa admiring our handiwork. Christmas music was playing on the radio. I had never been so contented.

Then Billy Joe looked at me and said, "Baby, I hate to do this, but I'm leaving tomorrow and will be out of town for the rest of the year."

I replied, "Billy Joe, you can't leave your tree." He just sat there looking at the tree.

"I've ordered your Christmas present," he said. "I'm having it shipped to Liz, along with all their presents. It should be there soon."

I said, "Billy Joe, if you won't be here for Christmas, then I'll give you your present tonight."

I got up from the sofa and went to the closet in the foyer. I had already wrapped his two presents, so I brought them to the living room.

I gave him the large one first. When he opened it and saw that it was an electric train, he said, "How did you know what I wanted?"

He got down on the floor, put it together, and we had fun playing with the train until almost midnight.

Finally, I asked him to open the other present. He did, and I would always remember the look on his face. He said, "Baby, I will leave the train under the tree tonight, but I'm taking this book to Aunt Aggie's so that I can keep it with my prized possessions. I don't ever want to misplace it."

I had given him a child's book, and on the dust cover, there was a little girl in a swing with a little boy pushing her. On the inside pages, the little boy and girl were playing on a slide, shooting marbles, and playing a lot of other children's games. I had written on the inside, "To Billy Joe, with whom I spent the happiest days of my life."

Later, as he was leaving, he hugged me so hard, I thought my back would break. After he was gone, I thought my heart would break.

A week before Christmas, on a Monday, the florist delivered a dozen red roses to my office. I was expecting the card to read "Merry Christmas." I opened it and saw the word "Love."

The following Sunday was Christmas Eve. I packed a bag and headed to Mother's for the night. Santa Claus always came there.

I stopped at Aunt Aggie's to give her a Christmas present before going on to Mother's. Aunt Aggie was happy to see me, and the first thing she said was, "I'm glad you came by today. A big box of Christmas presents from Billy Joe was sent to Liz all the way from Texas, and she brought yours over here. She thought you would be stopping by."

Aunt Aggie handed me a beautifully wrapped present. I opened it to find a navy skirt and jacket. The jacket was trimmed in red ribbing, and it zipped up the front. It was very casual. The Neiman Marcus card read, "Just a little something to wear to the grocery store."

I said, "Aunt Aggie, I don't know why he thinks I'm going to the grocery store. He knows I can't make chicken pot pie like you do. He's already told me that nobody can." Before I left, she insisted on giving me the recipe, just in case.

I got in the car and drove to Mother's. The whole family was there. Johnny was home from college, and Donna was there with her new husband, Jim.

After we ate and handed out presents, Aunt Maggie called. She asked Johnny to come down and put together a table and chairs. Her husband wasn't too handy at putting things together. Johnny asked me to go with him. He knew I would have fun at Maggie's.

On the way down, we laughed about the ugly tie I had given "the new husband." We had no way of knowing that it would be in style in another year and would become his favorite!

We walked in the door at Maggie's. The first thing she said was, "What are you doing here? I thought you'd be going back home tonight to see Billy Joe." I told her he was out of town.

She said she would bet anything he went out of town so that I could be at Mother's on Christmas Eve. I said, "You know I would have been here anyway. I've never missed Christmas Eve at Mother's."

We told her about the tie. I said, "Maggie, the truth is, I don't have one thing against Jim. It's just that he should have married Donna last year so their wedding would not have interfered with my life. That's why I gave him that ugly tie."

Johnny said, "Why don't you just forget about that wedding, Jane? You know how you are."

I smiled and said, "Yes, now I do. Billy Joe told me that I was just like everybody else. That I wanted people to like me; I wanted to be accepted. Billy Joe says that feeling rejected is the worst thing that can happen to a person."

Johnny replied, "I see." I think he did see. Since that Christmas Eve, I always felt accepted by Johnny.

Maggie finally sent the children to bed, and we started the Santa Workshop. The table was easy, but the chairs were difficult. We all worked on them. There was not enough hardware for all the chair parts, so we placed the leftover parts of one chair in the attic. It was after midnight.

On the way back to Mother's, Johnny sang, "All I want for Christmas is my two front teeth."

I was thinking that I already had all I wanted for Christmas—my family and Billy Joe.

21.

Dallas to Birmingham

Saturday night, the night before New Year's Eve, I had a call from Billy Joe. He was in Dallas and said he couldn't leave until Monday morning, so he asked me to fly down for New Year's Eve.

I flew into Dallas on Sunday evening. Billy Joe met me at the airport in a rental car. I asked how he got to Dallas, and he told me he rode with Harry.

When we arrived at the Executive Inn, he handed my bag to the bellhop and we went straight to the entertainment of the night—Ben Crane, a vocalist. He was good, but I had never heard of him. Billy Joe told me that Ben had been in prison and had worked for Glen Campbell when he was released. *Gentle on My Mind* was a big hit then. When the show was over, we went upstairs to a private party. There was plenty of food and more than enough to drink.

Billy Joe had said that he had driven out to Dallas with Harry, but I didn't see Harry at the party. I asked Billy Joe where he was, and he replied, "Harry had to work tonight." It was New Year's Eve. I couldn't understand what Harry would be doing on a holiday, but I didn't ask any more questions.

After the party, Billy Joe told me that our host, Ben Crane, had given him the room adjoining the party room. He said it was an accommodating room, but that there were so many at the party who didn't need to drive home that some of them were staying over. They were all in that room. He opened a door and I could hear people breathing and snoring. The light was on in the bathroom, and the door was cracked a little, so there was a faint light in the room.

I said, "I'm not sleeping in a room with all these other people."

Billy Joe said, "Well, the only other vacancy tonight is the hallway. Let's take a look." I didn't want to take a look. I had already seen the hallway. I could see my tote bag on a bed near the bathroom. I grabbed it, went into the bathroom, and put on my pajamas. I came back out and got in bed.

I couldn't get comfortable in that narrow bed. I didn't see how I would ever be able to go to sleep. There was silence in the room except for two people who snored occasionally.

Billy Joe said, in a loud whisper, "Quit squirming. These people will think we're doing it, and that would embarrass me to death."

"Don't turn the tables on me," I thought. I hit him on the arm.

He whispered loudly again, "No violence, please." We both giggled.

I heard the man in a bed in the corner say, "Damn." His wife giggled.

Early the next morning, the men were all up and out of there. That left the four of us females to get dressed. The woman sitting on the bed in the corner—the one who had giggled—was a bleached blonde about forty years old. She was applying her makeup with a lighted mirror so there were plenty of mirrors in the bathroom and bedroom for the rest of us.

She looked at me and smiled, then she said, "I just about died laughing at you two last night. I wanted to tell you it was okay, but I didn't want to further embarrass you. We're sacking out somewhere all the time 'cause in Dallas, Honey, you can't drink and drive anymore. The penalty is too high. And they didn't have another vacant room here. Ben didn't realize he would have all us locals staying over. We're all friends, anyway. We've known Billy Joe a long time. It's just that you didn't know us."

I said, "It was embarrassing, but I'm glad the men left first. If they were still here, I think I would have waited all day to be the last one up." They all laughed at that.

We had finished getting dressed when there was a knock on the door. It was Billy Joe with their husbands. All the wives started talking to him. They told him I was okay that morning.

Billy Joe said, "Well, I'm glad. I was afraid I'd be in the doghouse for the rest of the New Year." I didn't know why he said that. He had never been in the doghouse. But then, I had never slept in a room full of people.

We were all gathering our belongings and leaving. Laughing and talking, we rode down the elevator and said our good-byes at the front door. I had met them at the party the night before. I had met so many people that I couldn't recall all their names, but they all remembered my name.

The temperature was cold, and the wind was gusty. Billy Joe and I walked to the parking lot and got into his rental car. He told me he had to turn it in because we were riding back with Harry. At the airport rental agency, we met Harry. While Billy Joe was turning in his car, Harry was renting another one. It was a large white Chevrolet. Harry drove.

I sat in the back and read *Valley of the Dolls*. I had already seen the movie.

After riding for about ten or fifteen minutes, Harry stopped the car. I looked up and saw that we were at someone's basement door. I kept reading while they loaded some things in the trunk. Then we were off again.

We stopped and had lunch. Then we were on the road again. There was not much conversation made, and I was glad I didn't have to talk to Harry. I had failed to find any redeeming virtues in him. Harry lit a cigarette, and he was holding it so high that the smoke was making a film on the windshield. I was thinking about driving through that snowstorm for over four hours without a cigarette. It wasn't even snowing now, and Harry didn't crack the window. Perhaps that's the way some people treated rental cars. I just sat there and stared at Harry's window. Finally, I started reading again.

I had difficulty concentrating on the book, and I was not interested in the scenery. Billy Joe and I had driven through Texas and Oklahoma on previous trips. I remembered the first time I saw an oil derrick in the front yard of a somewhat large home in Oklahoma. I said, "Billy Joe, how gross! What kind of person would have something like that in their front yard?"

Billy Joe had replied, "A rich person. And if you had one in your front yard, you wouldn't think it was so ugly."

Billy Joe knew the history of Oklahoma. He said that the name Oklahoma meant red people. To the Choctaw Indians, "okla" meant people and "homma" meant red. He also told me that during the land rush in the late 1800s, some people were called "sooners" because they tried to stake claim on land "sooner" than they should have—before it was actually opened for claims. Oil was discovered in the late 1920s, but farmers had to vacate their land in the 1930s because of the drought. I did not know all the trivia, but I was familiar with a lot of the history myself. After all, wasn't I the one reading *The Grapes of Wrath* while my classmates were reading their history assignments?

I asked him if Sutter's Creek was in Oklahoma. He laughed and said, "Where did you ever come up with an idea like that?" I knew I was wrong, because every time he disagreed with me, or when I was wrong about something, he would ask, "Where did you ever come up with an idea like that?"

Then he started telling me about California and the gold rush. He finally got to the part about Sutter's Creek being in California.

I didn't know where he got all his information, but he knew more about history than anyone I had ever known. Riding around with him was one history lesson after another. I had never liked the subject of history in school, but Billy Joe enjoyed telling me things I didn't already know. I asked questions—just to hear him talk.

I had fun riding around the countryside with Billy Joe even though most people would wonder what I was doing in Texas with him. In 1967, a young lady did not run around the country with a man unless she was married to him, so there was no way I could talk about my trips and all the things I had learned.

I certainly could not discuss it with my family. I still remembered New Year's Day in 1961 when I had moved from Overton to Atlanta. Lucky and his wife, Gina, had visited us that day. I was telling Gina about my plans to move to Atlanta and attend business school. She asked me to move in with them. So I loaded my clothes in their car, and when they were ready to leave, I got in the car. Mother knew I was moving, but Daddy must have thought I was going to Lucky's for a visit. I said goodbye to everyone. Mother said something to Daddy as Lucky backed out of the driveway. Daddy walked toward the car, shaking his finger at us, saying, "You're not going anywhere, young lady." Lucky just laughed and kept backing out of the driveway.

Donna ran back into the house. I found out later that she was in a hurry to rearrange the bedroom we had shared. She was so happy to have a room of her own minus all my sewing items and books scattered around that she couldn't wait for us to get out of the driveway.

I knew Daddy would do more than shake a finger if he thought I was riding around the country with Billy Joe. I thought it was okay to be with Billy Joe, but it just didn't look proper to be riding around with Billy Joe and Harry. I knew they were up to no good. Billy Joe knew I should not have been there, and that was the reason he was acting nervous. I was beginning to see that Daddy could have a valid point about some of my actions.

I was not learning anything on this trip. The only thing I could think about was Harry and the fact that we were riding with him. Somewhere during that ride, I understood what Al had been trying to tell me. Realization had dawned. Billy Joe had his life, and I had mine. We did live in two different worlds. I wished Billy Joe had sent me back to Atlanta on a plane from Dallas.

On the way, Harry made two more stops. Both times, he removed something from the trunk. I had no idea what was in the trunk, and I didn't want to know what was in the trunk. Billy Joe had said to me several times, "What you don't know won't hurt you." I thought it was "for the best," as Billy Joe would say, that I didn't ask any questions. If Billy Joe had wanted me to know what was in the trunk, he would have told me.

Wilson Pickett was singing *The Midnight Hour* on the radio. Billy Joe didn't even sing along in Harry's presence. I wondered if Harry knew Billy Joe could sing. He probably didn't. If Harry knew Billy Joe sang to me, he would perceive that as a weakness. Billy Joe acted tough in Harry's presence, but I knew he really was not as tough as he acted—at least not to me.

It was easy to pretend I was reading so that I wouldn't be prone to make conversation. All I had to do was stare at the pages of the book.

We were in Alabama when I shut the book and placed it on the seat. At dusk, Harry turned onto a road that seemed to be going up a mountain. Billy Joe said to me, "We have to stop here. And you need to get out, too."

A mansion was situated at the top of the hill. I asked, "Who lives here?" Billy Joe told me it was the home of a politician.

I couldn't think of a single politician who lived in Alabama. There were some on my list of contacts at the office, but I couldn't remember their names. Billy Joe would have told me more if Harry had not been there.

Several men were sitting on the second level glassed-in portion of a deck that wrapped around the back of the house. They greeted us as we got out of the car and started up the steps. At the top of the steps, one of the men asked if I would like to join the ladies inside. He opened a door to the den. Two older ladies walked toward us. He introduced me to Helen and Betty. Helen asked me to have a seat.

I heard the men walk down to the car, open the trunk and close it. It sounded as if they went to the basement. I didn't really want to know, but I still wondered what was in the trunk. Billy Joe had told me one time that if it were not for all the legitimate people with lots of money, there would be no market for his high-end merchandise, and he would be out of business. And he said that his customers were some of the same people sitting in the front pews in church every Sunday. I could visualize the men on the deck sitting in the front pews.

Meanwhile, the ladies tried to make conversation with me. They talked about how mild the weather had been on New Year's Day. I wanted to tell them how cold and windy it had been in Dallas, but for some reason, I didn't want to talk about Billy Joe and where we had been.

Helen brought me a cup of coffee. It was too hot and I didn't want to ask for an ice cube. I did ask where the bathroom was. Betty pointed down a hallway and said, "Second door on the left."

I had never seen a bathroom decorated so attractively. The shower curtain was certainly different from my plain plastic liner at home. I didn't like all those do-dads on the counter, but they looked appropriate in that house. They must have spent hundreds of dollars decorating the bathroom.

I returned to the den, and before I had time to drink my coffee, Billy Joe came in and asked, "Are you ready to go?"

I got up from the sofa and said, "I'm ready when you are." Looking at the ladies, I smiled and thanked them for the coffee. Then we left.

Back in the car, Harry glanced at Billy Joe and said, "We have only one more stop." They talked about furs and the quality of some of them. I didn't know anything about furs. I couldn't tell one from another except by the color. Phoebe had a mink, but I knew she would owe Rich's for the rest of her life. She had to pay to have it stored and cleaned every summer.

I was glad I did not have to pay that much to have my cashmere coat cleaned. I needed to have it cleaned now, and I said, "Billy Joe, do you have any laundry that needs to be picked up at Mac and Jac's this week? I'm taking my coat there to have it cleaned. I could have it cleaned downstairs, but I would rather take it to Mac and Jac's."

Harry said, "Why do you wear that old black coat all the time? Wouldn't you like to have a fur? I can arrange it."

"I don't need a fur, Harry. If a cloth coat is good enough for Jackie Kennedy, it's good enough for me."

Harry turned and glanced at me. Then he said, "Where did you hear something like that?"

"I saw it on television. Don't you ever look at anything educational?"

"I wouldn't call that educational," said Harry. "I'm educated in furs. A fur could give you more class."

"Harry, if you were educated in furs, you would know that having a fur doesn't mean you have class. It just means you have a fur!"

Harry started another sentence, but Billy Joe interrupted him by saying, "I don't have anything at Mac and Jac's this week."

I knew why Billy Joe had interrupted Harry. He could see that Harry and I were getting ready to match wits. Billy Joe wouldn't like that, so I didn't say anything else.

Billy Joe had said a few weeks ago that he wished I would put forth more effort to get along with Harry. He said, "Sometimes you can have a 'smart mouth,' but I ignore it. Harry won't ignore it."

He said it looked like Harry and I were attacking each other in such a subtle way that no one else seemed to notice. Billy Joe couldn't pinpoint the problem, but he thought there was always an uncompromising situation between Harry and me. He said, "It puts a strain on me because I feel like I have to defend you, and I don't even know what for."

The next time I was in Harry's presence, I was amicable. Even I couldn't believe how easy it had been. Later, Billy Joe pointed out that my being agreeable with Harry was exaggerated, and anybody could see that it was all "put on."

"In fact," Billy Joe said, "people can tell a mile away that it's phony. I can't understand why you want to ask him questions like, 'How have you been, Harry?' and 'Don't you think it's lovely weather, Harry?' Why are you doing that, Baby? Never before have you asked Harry how he's been."

I sat and pondered on that one. I had decided to be pleasant to Harry, and now Billy Joe didn't like that either.

I wanted to tell Billy Joe that I preferred not to be in Harry's company anymore, but I knew that would be impossible. I was afraid he would choose Harry over me, only because I had to go to work every day. I was happier when it was just the two of us.

Finally, I told Billy Joe that I was pleasant to Harry because he didn't like me, and I was afraid of him. Billy Joe indicated that there was no reason for me to be afraid of Harry. He said Harry liked me okay, but if the truth were known, Harry was more afraid of me than I was of him. I asked why, and Billy Joe said, "Because you are not one of us, and he thinks you know too much."

Billy Joe had told me some of the lawless things Harry had done, but I knew that it was all hearsay. Billy Joe had informed me that if a person heard something, and they had nothing to back it up, it was just "hearsay." After working with attorneys, I knew "hearsay" would never hold up in court. So I didn't know why Harry was worried about me. What would I tell?

These conversations with Billy Joe concerning Harry were upsetting to me. I didn't know how much more of Harry I could tolerate. I was apprehensive in Harry's presence, and I certainly couldn't condone his questionable activities.

Even though I was also feeling fearful about Billy Joe, at that time, I still hoped he would always be above reproach. I decided to just sit still and hope for a miracle.

That had been a few weeks ago. And now we were riding through Birmingham in Harry's rental car. Harry made a three turns and then drove down a street lined with small brick houses. He stopped the car in a driveway. A big black man came out the door.

Harry got out of the car, opened the trunk, and removed a sheet that had something bulky in it. He said to the man, "Here's all that's left. See what you can do with it." The man nodded his head, took the big sheet, and went back in the house. Harry got in the car and we drove off.

As we entered the main highway, Harry asked Billy Joe if he wanted to drive. Billy Joe said, "No."

I was tired of reading, so I said, "I'll drive."

Harry said, "You can't drive this car."

I had been quiet long enough. "Yes, I can. I know how to drive. Billy Joe lets me drive his car all the time. Don't you, Billy Joe? And this is just a plain white rental car."

Harry said, "No, this is not a plain white rental car; it's a stolen white rental car."

I had seen Harry rent the car, so I couldn't believe it was stolen. He just didn't want me to drive.

Billy Joe opened the glove compartment and took out the papers. He looked at the papers, and then he glared at Harry. He said, "You didn't!" Harry just glared back at him.

Billy Joe said, "Take us to the airport."

Harry said, "Damn, here we go again. She's either gonna have to get in or get out."

Billy Joe said, "She's getting out."

Harry drove to the airport in Birmingham. It was a good thing I wasn't driving. I could not have found the airport in the dark.

Harry pulled up to the curb at the airport. He threw the gear lever into the Park position and leaned his head back on the seat. Then he took a deep breath and let it out slowly and loudly.

I stuffed my book into the tote bag. Billy Joe and I got out of the car and headed to the ticket counter. After he had purchased my ticket, I said, "What's wrong with Harry? Why is he acting like this?" There was no answer.

I said, "That car couldn't be stolen. I saw him rent it."

Billy Joe replied, "Yes, you did. On a bogus credit card."

He escorted me to the gate and said, "I'm sorry, Baby." He gave me a quick hug, and then he walked away. I could tell he was uptight. There was no warmth in his hug.

When Billy Joe was under pressure, he would usually squeeze my hand. But he couldn't do that while he sat in the front seat with Harry. The night had been awkward and unpleasant for me, and it was all Harry's fault.

I stood there, bewildered at what had happened. Billy Joe had never acted quite like that before. But then, it wasn't unusual for his demeanor to make a drastic change when Harry was around. I could tell when Billy Joe was tense. He would hold his teeth together and the muscle in his jaw would get solid. I had noticed him doing that a couple of times before, and it was always when Harry was there.

Billy Joe and I had established a line of communication the night we met. He had been perfectly honest when he told me of the good and bad things in his past and how he felt about life in general. He had even told me of some of his friends' outrageous shenanigans, revealing things I didn't want to know and certainly didn't need to know. And I had flooded his mind with my pet peeves and aggravations. Suddenly I felt disjointed. In a single day, somewhere between Dallas and Birmingham, that line of communication had been broken.

Fortunately, I had to wait only forty-five minutes before boarding the plane to Atlanta. While in the air, I checked to see how much cash there was in my bag. For the first time, Billy Joe had forgotten to give me cab fare.

During the next two months, Billy Joe was on the phone with me almost daily. He returned to Atlanta on the weekends at least every two weeks, staying a day or two each time. His mood was quiet, and he appeared to be preoccupied. Neither one of us mentioned Harry.

He was constantly holding my hand and hugging me. Each time he was back, the radio was on, and the music played, but I didn't hear Billy Joe sing a single note. And then he would leave again.

22.

The Rude Awakening

The bus stopped in front of my office building. I stepped off into the bitter, gusty wind. The weatherman had been right—winter was having one last fling. So was my black cashmere coat. Stopping in the coffee shop to get a doughnut, I saw Tim Hopkins, the new guy in my building. He and another man were sitting at a table in the corner.

Tim and his partners had opened an office on my floor before Christmas. Tim had told me they ran a business management company. There were initials on the door to their office.

Tim and I had talked many times at the elevators and in the coffee shop. He was such a friendly person that some of the girls working on my floor had asked him to join the bowling team. He didn't join the team, but he had shown up at the Rodeway piano bar several times. All the members of the team liked Tim. His voice was good, and he enjoyed singing. Tim told us he learned to sing in church.

One night Phoebe met us at the Rodeway. Tim stopped by, too. He was talking about a white cottage-type house with a picket fence that he had seen in Decatur, and asked if I would like to go take a look at it. He said that he wanted to buy it, but it was not on the market.

Finally, two of the girls on the bowling team said that we should all go, so he would stop talking about it. Phoebe said, "Sounds like a good idea to me." The four of us got into Tim's car and he drove to Decatur.

He stopped the car in front of a small white frame house and began talking about that house being exactly what he was looking for. He kept looking at me. Then he asked if I had ever seen a house like that before.

I told him I didn't think so. I couldn't understand why he would want that house. The fence needed repairs, and the house looked rather shabby to me from what I could see with only one streetlight burning two doors away. During the ride back to the Rodeway, Tim was unusually quiet.

It was getting late, and the other members of the bowling team had already gone home, so we didn't go back inside. Phoebe and I stood near our cars and talked for a little while. We laughed about the house in Decatur. I told Phoebe that it was difficult for me to understand why Tim would want a house in Decatur. I didn't know anybody who lived there, except maybe Slot. Harry and Billy Joe had gone to DeKalb County one time, but I didn't know if they went to Decatur. After chatting a while, we got in our cars and drove away.

Another time, I was working late in the office and ran into Tim at the elevators on my way out. He asked me to have dinner with him next door at Pitty Pat's Porch. During dinner, we talked about growing up. I learned that he grew up in his grandmother's house. He told me they attended church every Sunday, and she had insisted that he take piano lessons when he was a boy.

He asked all about my childhood, my jobs, and what I did in my spare time. I told him about growing up in a small town, sewing, and taking piano lessons. I also talked about working for Mr. Phillips before I started working for Mr. Green, and how the grass had not been greener until now.

He asked about the tall guy with black hair who met me sometimes at Davison's for lunch. I said he was a friend from Overton and that we had gone to the same church when we grew up. Billy Joe usually wore one of his Alpaca sweaters or his black wool overcoat when we would meet for lunch. I was always proud of his appearance.

After dinner that night, Tim offered to drop me off at the apartment since I had taken the bus to work that morning. When he stopped the car in front of my apartment building, he said he would like to try that piano of mine one day to see if he could still play.

One afternoon at five o'clock, I was waiting for the elevator to go downstairs. When the door opened, Tim stepped out. He said he thought his boss was still in the office and asked if I had time to drop in and meet him. He had previously mentioned that he would like for his boss to meet me. We went to his office, but the door was locked, and his boss had gone for the day. I was surprised when I looked in and saw the sparsely furnished office. There was a table, two chairs, and a two-drawer file cabinet. But I knew how long it could take to get furniture delivered. Tim said he was sorry his boss was gone, but maybe we could meet another time. On the way home, I wondered when their furniture would arrive.

Coffee and doughnut in hand, I pressed the button for the elevator as Tim rounded the corner. We spoke and boarded the elevator going up. Tim had a serious look on his face. On the way up, he turned to me and said that his boss would be in town later in the day, and he asked if they could drop by my office at five o'clock. For some reason, he still wanted his boss to meet me. Mr. Green was out of town, so I told Tim it would be okay.

They arrived promptly at five o'clock. Tim's boss was a short, stocky-built man wearing a dark suit. His first name was Bob. I didn't catch the last name. We chatted about how cold it was, traveling by car, bus and plane, and other unimportant things.

Then Tim said, "Jane, do you remember the house in Decatur that we went to see one night after bowling?"

I answered, "Yes, why? You made such a big deal of it, I thought you would have purchased it by now. Just go up, ring the doorbell, and ask if they will sell it to you. You can save the real estate commission by doing that. If they won't sell, then go find another one." The three of us laughed.

A few minutes later, Bob's eyebrow manifested an unmistakable tilt as he said, "Tim, I have to go now. I think you may be right on this one.

I'll talk to you later. Jane, it's been a real pleasure meeting you." And with that, Bob left.

Déjà vu. I had always been conscious of eyebrows, and I had encountered Bob's eyebrow somewhere before, but where? His eyebrow seemed so strangely and intensely familiar that a feeling of queasiness swept over me.

As the door closed, Tim turned to me and said, "Jane, there's an investigation going on." He showed me a badge, but my eyes could not focus on the words. Tim told me he was a special agent and there were some long-named agencies working with the FBI, GBI, and other names I couldn't remember.

Everything else was a blur as he talked about my frequent trips with Billy Joe. I didn't know what to say, so I said nothing. He asked no questions.

My eyes were focused on Tim's mouth. I tried to comprehend what he was saying about the house in Decatur and my observations. He was talking about Billy Joe and his friends being suspects in a number of burglaries. He said it was a big operation spanning several states, and they intended to get to the bottom of it.

Tim said, "Billy Joe's not a petty thief. Being a booster is what is does in his spare time for entertainment. He's a BTO. In case you don't know, that means Big Time Operator—scams and shams, stocks and bonds, and any number of racketeering activities. Those people can dismantle an alarm system and crack a safe. They can clean out an entire jewelry store or clothing store, and no one notices until the next morning."

After hearing that Billy Joe was a Big Time Operator, I was not proud of the accusations, but frankly, I found myself feeling relieved to hear that he was the best. It would be an embarrassment to him for people to think he was just another petty thief. Even my daddy had said, "Be the best at whatever you are."

Tim described Billy Joe and his associates as being ruthless and vicious criminals. Billy Joe was not like that at all. He was kind and sensitive. He acted tough on the outside, but on the inside he was still that unwanted teenager in pursuit of acceptance. I knew him well. Tim didn't know Billy Joe at all.

He told me that Billy Joe and Harry worked together a lot and that Renee traveled. He said Renee was a prostitute and Harry was a pimp, burglar and con artist from Texas. I thought that maybe he did have a Texas drawl. I had determined they were not from Atlanta, but Harry seemed to be everywhere. I had never thought about where they lived. In fact, I had never thought about them at all except when Harry was around.

He said that he did not understand why Billy Joe drove everywhere he went. He told me that for a long period of time, Billy Joe would take a flight out of Atlanta every Monday morning and return on Friday. Then one day he had stopped. Tim said that they had not seen him board a plane in years. He told me that Billy Joe was good at what he did; he had been a suspect numerous times, but had been found guilty only once. That got my attention. I looked at him questioningly. He said, "Billy Joe is known from coast to coast as a jewel thief."

Billy Joe himself had told me that was what he did. Even though I didn't see the evidence, I had witnessed the adrenaline rush. I had also gathered enough information from his conversations with Harry to make me believe he was involved in burglaries and other wrongful deeds connected with Harry.

Tim mentioned my flying in and out of Atlanta on the weekends. Because of my close association with Billy Joe, Tim said I had been under close scrutiny. They thought I would lead them to the answers to a lot of their questions.

Then I considered what Milton Riggs had said to me at the funeral home that day. "If you get into anything away from Overton, there's not a damn thing I can do to help you." I didn't want his help. I did not know what I had gotten into, but I knew I had done nothing wrong.

I was relieved when Tim said, "I think I have finally convinced Bob that you have no real knowledge of what is going on."

I wondered what Tim meant by "real" knowledge. At one time, Billy Joe thought I had no real knowledge of what was going on, but Billy Joe had thought I didn't pay attention to detail. I only knew what Billy Joe had told me, and at one time, I really thought he was more entertaining than truthful.

If I ever truly admitted to myself what I thought was going on, I knew I would have to make a decision. And that was one decision I didn't want to make. I needed Billy Joe, and he needed me. It was that simple.

Then Tim said to me, "Tell me, please, exactly what does Billy Joe mean to you?" The question shocked me. I gave Tim an icy stare. I had never really thought about it before; I had taken Billy Joe for granted. Ours was a bond that I could neither define nor explain.

At that moment I realized Billy Joe meant everything to me. Billy Joe gave me my self-confidence, my flippant attitude, and my enthusiasm for life itself. My icy stare was frozen on Tim as the tears poured down my face. But my features remained as stoic as when he first asked me the question.

Finally, Tim looked down at the floor, then reached in his pocket and handed me his handkerchief as he said, "It's already dark outside, so I will drop you off, but I suggest you try to stay away from Billy Joe and his friends. It's not to your advantage to be in their company. It was never my intent to question you, but I felt you should be warned."

I was glad he had not questioned me. My granddaddy had always said, "You can go to hell for lying, just like you can for stealing." I did not intend to lie; I did not intend to say anything.

Tim drove me home. He pulled up in front of my building. As I opened the car door, Special Agent Tim Hopkins said to me, "I want you to know that I don't really believe you are totally innocent of all knowledge of what's going on, but I have convinced my boss that you are innocent. I just wish I had somebody like you in my corner, Jane. You'll be okay."

Innocent? Of course I was innocent. I wondered how I could be guilty
of anything. The only thing I had done was ride—in cars and in planes.
Billy Joe had said that if I didn't know something for a fact, then I didn't
know it at all. And the things Billy Joe had told me were just "hearsay."

When I opened the apartment door, the phone was ringing. It was
Billy Joe. He said, "Jane, I need to tell you something, and I don't have
long to talk, so listen carefully. I want you to go to Phoebe's and stay a
week, or maybe two. Get out of that apartment now. Don't talk to
anyone. I will call you at work. You know I would never do anything to
hurt you, Baby." I heard a dial tone. Billy Joe had hung up the phone.

As I replaced the receiver, I thought, "But I already have, Billy Joe."
Then I remembered that I had not talked to anyone. Tim had done all
the talking. And there was no way Billy Joe could possibly know about
Tim and his boss.

"To whom was he referring?" I wondered. Then I realized that I was
not afraid of the FBI; I was afraid of Harry. My life was falling apart, and
somehow I thought Harry was to blame. My mind was spinning. I
wanted out of there.

I called Phoebe and asked if I could stay with her a few days. I
explained briefly what had happened.

Phoebe said, "You're upset. I'll come over and help you pack."

By then, I was crying again. I picked up the phone and dialed
Mother's number. When she answered the phone, I said, "Mother, is it
okay if I move back home?"

She replied, "I'll have to ask your daddy; why do you want to do that?"

I said, "He always said that one day I would come to a rude
awakening. Just tell him I did."

She asked, and I heard Daddy say, "I guess so."

Immediately after hanging up the phone, I was sorry I had called
Mother. What would Billy Joe do without me? What would I do without
him? Why did I have to act first, and think later?

I wondered what Daddy really thought. I had never kept things from Mother. In fact, I had told her I was seeing Billy Joe. She told Daddy, and that probably prompted Daddy and Milton Riggs to get busy checking out everything Billy Joe was doing.

During the summer, before Donna's wedding, I asked Mother what Daddy had said about my seeing Billy Joe. She told me he would never admit to me that he knew anything about it. I asked her why, and she said that Daddy told her if he admitted he knew, then he would be forced to do something about it. And he didn't know what to do, short of killing me, since I was over twenty-one.

Could it be a family trait? Daddy pretended I wasn't seeing Billy Joe, and I pretended Billy Joe was doing nothing wrong.

Phoebe was on the way over, and I had to get my things together to leave. I pulled a Franklin Simon shopping bag off the closet shelf for my shoes. The Franklin Simon shopping bag! My stomach felt queasy again. Then I remembered where I had seen Bob and his uplifted eyebrow. On the day I took the dresses down to Al's in a Franklin Simon shopping bag, Bob and another man were standing at the elevator when I returned with a sandwich from the deli. I knew I had seen that eyebrow somewhere. Were they waiting and watching to see what I would do that day? I was glad I had left early instead of leaving at twelve o'clock. At twelve, they could have followed me home, and then Al would have seen *my* name in the paper. Possession of stolen goods was against the law, and I was guilty, but I remembered Billy Joe telling me what he heard someone say one time. "If you're accused of stealing a train, and the whistle is still in your pocket—deny, deny, deny." If asked, I probably would not deny it, but since I had not caused the problem, I did not see how mentioning the dresses to anyone would solve it.

Phoebe arrived and helped me pack, then we drove to her apartment. We sat in the den drinking hot chocolate. There was not a lot to say. Reaching in my bag, I located my cigarettes and the 14K gold Dunhill lighter that Billy Joe had given me.

I remembered what Billy Joe had said about that lighter. Looking at the lighter, I said to Phoebe, "Well, I guess I'll have to get another lighter. Billy Joe bought this one for me one night at Rich's. He said it had an automatic control on it and would only light up every forty-five minutes. I think I need one that lights up more often."

I rambled on. "He didn't like for me to smoke too much. I had to wait for him to light my cigarette, and sometimes he would make me wait forever. He would start to light it, then he would stop and talk. He would do this so many times that I believed he was just postponing every cigarette. On his face, I would see that look of his, and that little mischievous grin."

I sat there and cried.

Phoebe knew there was nothing she could say to make me feel better, and I felt too exhausted to talk anymore. Phoebe went to bed. I sat there for a long time before I finally turned in for the night.

Phoebe and I were up early, and we dressed for work in near silence. I felt like everything was running in slow motion. I wondered how that could be possible when everything had been moving so fast the night before.

The traffic was heavy and I was worried about being late for work. After the long bumper-to-bumper drive down Peachtree, I finally reached downtown.

As soon as I was in the office, I called Al. He had no invoicing for me to do, but I asked him if I could come down and bring my lunch at noontime.

Al said, "Anytime, come on down."

At 12:15, I walked in the door of Al's shop. I cleared a place on the cluttered desk and opened the bag containing my sandwich from the deli. Trying to appear aloof, I said, "Maybe I should have brought a cake for the celebration."

Al wanted to know what I was celebrating.

I said, "Not for my celebration—for yours, Al."

I told him all about Tim Hopkins. Al looked at me in disbelief and said, "I can't believe you were seeing an FBI man. Billy Joe would be upset if he knew that."

"But, Al," I protested. "I wasn't really 'seeing' him. He's just somebody who works in my building, and he's always around after bowling. I had dinner with him a couple of times after work, but that was because ours paths crossed on the way out the door. You know I don't see anybody except Billy Joe."

Al said, "I know that, but Billy Joe might not see things the way I do, considering the circumstances."

I said, "Well, Billy Joe has mentioned that he thought I was too friendly with people I didn't know. Now I understand what he meant. But I've always been friendly to people, and Billy Joe says that he wants me to go out more and be a well-rounded person. How was I to know that the guy was with the FBI? Besides, I've never had any reason to avoid the FBI, and I don't want to start avoiding them now."

Then I told Al about Billy Joe's phone call the previous night, and of my decision to move back home. Al stood there and listened. Finally, he said, "You've done a good job keeping your two lives separate. But it's difficult for Billy Joe to keep them separate any longer. It's time for you to move on. You've been Billy Joe's lifeline and safe harbor for almost a year now. I know this parting will be difficult for both of you. I will still worry about you."

"Al, you don't have to worry about me," I replied. "Billy Joe's been preparing me for this since my sister's wedding, when he told me he couldn't see me anymore. He's been telling me for a long time that he wants me to get on with my life. I knew this day would come; I just didn't know when. And I never thought I would be the one leaving. I'm okay; I'm just tired."

My voice broke. I was crying again. I didn't want Al to see me cry; I wanted him to think I was tough. But I was tired—tired of worrying about Billy Joe and completely worn out from pretending everything was okay. I wanted to tell Al that our two worlds didn't collide; they just ended.

Al said, "Don't get weepy on me. I don't know what to do with a weepy woman." Then he walked over to the two-color press and shuffled a few boxes. I heard him blow his nose.

I thought he would be happy that I would not be seeing Billy Joe anymore, but Al acted sad when I left. He patted me on the back as I headed toward the door.

I called the movers and made arrangements to move the following Saturday. Then I notified Mrs. Atwood. She was sorry I had to move, but she informed me that they had a waiting list for an apartment the size of mine. She said she didn't think I would have to pay the rent much longer.

That's how I ended up back in Overton.

The initials on Tim Hopkins' office door disappeared, and I never saw him again.

Billy Joe called me at work a week later. I told him I had moved, and that I couldn't see him anymore. He said, "Where did you ever come up with an idea like that?"

He gave a nervous laugh. Then, in a soft voice, he said, "I understand, Baby. It's for the best."

He said he would talk with me later. After hanging up the phone, I sat at my desk and cried again. In my mind, I questioned my actions. Other people had arguments before parting. Billy Joe and I had never spoken angry words. I was vacillating between being relieved to get away from the pressure and being sorry I had moved.

The next day I called Blanche to bring her up to date. She suggested we have dinner on Friday night. I said, "Fine, why don't we meet at Mama Mia's?" I could think of nowhere else that would be more appropriate.

Blanche was in a somber mood on Friday night. She enlightened me on a number of things Billy Joe and Harry had managed to accomplish. All of it was illegal. She had known Billy Joe and some of his associates for the past eight years. She was aware of more than I could imagine, but she had never talked about it because she needed her job. She told me that working in bars at night had taught her to shut her eyes and do her work.

She said Billy Joe tried to protect me from his other life—that he had an uncanny ability to sense when it was necessary to remove me from a situation.

"I know he did, Blanche." I told her there had been several hard-to-explain, sometimes upsetting occurrences. In particular, there was my cause for alarm in Texas the week before Thanksgiving. I was wearing an off-white dress with rhinestone buttons down the front. We were attending a party at a large hotel. Billy Joe walked up to me, holding my purse and black cashmere coat on his arm.

He took my hand and said, "Let's go." Escorting me to the elevator, Billy Joe handed me several large bills from his money clip. After pressing the "down" button, he told me to go downstairs and take a cab to the airport.

I asked, "What about my tote bag?"

He placed his index finger to his lips. That meant, "Hush and listen." He said, "I'll bring it when I come." The elevator stopped. As I was getting on the elevator, Billy Joe turned and opened the door to the stairway. He was leaving, too.

I needed my tote bag, but it was back at the hotel where we were staying, so there was no way I could retrieve it. The weather was too mild to be wearing a coat, but I would have to cover the party dress all the way home to keep people from staring at those rhinestone buttons. I had not given that strange incident another thought after Billy Joe returned my bag the following week. I told Blanche that Harry was not even in Texas at the time it happened.

I did not admit to Blanche that I was afraid of Harry, but I told her I could not understand Billy Joe's association with Harry. She said that for the past several years, Harry and Renee had acted as Billy Joe's substitute family and that they had stood by him through thick and thin. Billy Joe was loyal to his friends.

I said, "Blanche, I know how they feel about Billy Joe, but Harry and Renee don't particularly like me. Renee told me when Billy Joe was in jail that I was an encumbrance to him. And why does he act uneasy when I'm around his friends?"

She replied, "No, you have not been an encumbrance to Billy Joe, but I believe you are to his friends. They don't know what to say or how to act when you're around, and that makes Billy Joe feel uneasy. It's not a good situation for any of you.

"When you first started seeing Billy Joe, I thought you were as blind as a bat and as dumb as a doorknob. Then I could see you were neither. But you just don't fit in with them. Harry and Renee like you fine, Janie, but they know you could never adapt to the way they live. And you know it, too."

I wasn't shocked at anything Blanche told me. I was no longer in denial, but I was still numb from it all. I did not care to hear about Billy Joe's bad qualities. I understood the essence of Billy Joe—his strengths and his weaknesses. I knew his basic nature was good. And that's the only thing that mattered to me.

Blanche and I had sat in this same booth less than a year ago. My heart had been broken then. I thought a heart could break only once. The recurring queasy feeling was in the pit of my stomach. I couldn't bear the thought of being away from Billy Joe, but I had done what I thought was best. Billy Joe had been right about my "getting on with my life," but neither one of us would let go.

I was thinking how brave Blanche had been when she was younger and her husband had left her all alone with a new baby. Somehow other people seemed to move on, and I knew I would, too.

Blanche said that even though I was hurting inside, she was proud of the way I was conducting myself. She said I was showing maturity. And before we left, she reached over, placed her hand on my arm and said, "Janie, you will forget, in time."

23.

The Final Goodbye

Overton was the same small town it had always been. Nothing had changed. One Saturday, I felt the walls closing in at home, so I drove around in the car. I had been gone from Overton seven years and had no close association with anyone there. Friends from high school who had not moved away were married and had children, so we had very little in common and had not kept in close touch.

My two allies were still in town—Mrs. Garrison at the restaurant, and Miss Lillie, the county bailiff. I had not seen them in such a long time that I was embarrassed to show up at their door.

I stopped at the restaurant first. I seated myself in a booth, and a waitress came over and took my order for a piece of chocolate pie. Mrs. Garrison came out of the kitchen and saw me sitting there. She smiled, walked over to the booth and sat down. "I figured you'd be by here sooner or later," she said.

"I've moved back," I told her.

"I knew you had, probably before the movers arrived. And I know you've got your things scattered all over town—boxes in one basement and furniture in another. You know how word travels in a small town. You're a grown woman now. I hope your daddy won't be calling out here checking on you like he did when you were a teenager."

I asked, "What do you mean?"

"I never told you, but sometimes at night, he would call. When I answered the phone, he would say, 'Mae, tell Jane to come home.'"

In His Corner

"He didn't give me a chance to say whether or not you were here before he hung up the phone. I always said a little prayer that you would get home soon. I never mentioned it to you. I knew you couldn't be too far away, and you always managed to get home just in the nick of time."

"Well, I never left the county. But I did have some close calls when I was supposed to be at church and one of my friends from church would phone me before I got home. Why didn't he just call his friend, Milton Riggs, and ask him where I was? Milton kept up with everybody in town back then."

We sat and laughed at how things used to be, and then I told her I was going to see Miss Lillie. As I got up to leave, Mrs. Garrison said, "It's good to have you back."

I got in the car and drove to the courthouse square. Parking in front of the drug store, I looked up and saw that Miss Lillie had the window open. Miss Lillie owned half the stores on the square, and she would sit in her little office upstairs, knitting and collecting the rent. I raced up the stairs and knocked on her door. She said, "The door's open. Come on in."

I walked in, and there she sat. She was knitting. The cigarette in her mouth had ashes an inch long. There were ashes on the front of her dress. The soft curls in her gray hair indicated that she had a new permanent, and she still wore the heavy gold coins dangling from her pierced ears. Her "pocketbook," as she called it, was by the chair. It was a huge thing, and it looked almost like a knitting bag. I knew that pocketbook contained a bottle of vodka and her .38 Smith & Wesson. She carried those two items everywhere.

I said to her, "Is that all you've got to do? Sit here and knit?"

People called her a "tough old bird." And she was. She just looked at me as she sat there knitting. Finally she said, "It's about time you got here. Where in the hell have you been? Don't you know I've been worried about you? And your poor mama has already turned gray-headed in the past year. I've saved your butt many a time, but this time I thought your daddy would really kill you if he could get his hands on you. Milton Riggs has been running around here like a chicken with its head cut off."

"Why is Milton doing that?" I asked.

"He's worried about you, too. He's more concerned than he was the day you stole that car parked in front of the drug store."

I started laughing. Then I said, "I just left Mrs. Garrison. I told her I was stopping by to see you. I started to come by to ask if you wanted to ride out there with me, but you told me the day we stole the car that you would never get in the car with me again."

She didn't comment, so I continued, "And to set the record straight, I didn't steal the car. It was an honest mistake. It's not my fault that my key fit that man's car. Daddy had told me he would leave the car parked in front of the drug store. And when I stopped by here and asked you to go to lunch, we walked out and got in the car. It was identical to my new car. And the key fit. You know what they say, 'If the key fits, drive it.' The only indication I had that the car wasn't mine was when I reached to turn on the radio as we drove back from Garrison's restaurant, and I saw that it didn't have a radio."

Miss Lillie said, "Well you need to learn to pay more attention to things."

I said, "Miss Lillie, if there's one thing I've learned in the past seven years, it's to pay attention to detail. And I'm glad you taught me to knit. I've knitted a red bag for my makeup. You should be proud of me."

"I've always been proud of you," she said. "I just wish you wouldn't worry me so much."

We sat and talked for over an hour. As I got up to leave, I told her that I was sorry I had worried her so much and that I would never do it again. In fact, just to make her laugh, I told her that I planned to marry a nice man who went to church every Sunday, and we would live happily ever after.

She did laugh, and then she said, "Don't go to the extreme."

Bouncing down the steps to the sidewalk, I was in such a good mood that I thought, "I have one more stop to make." I opened the door and walked into the drug store. Martha was behind the counter smoking a cigarette. She gave me the same stare she had always given me.

I stepped up to the counter and said, "Martha, fix me a milkshake!"

She put the cigarette in an ashtray, shook her head and said, "Damn you. Now I'll have to wash the blender. I wish to hell you'd go back to Atlanta."

Martha hated making milkshakes and washing the blender, and she knew I really didn't want one. "It's good to see you, too," I said, as I laughed all the way out the door. She was probably still grumbling as I got in the car.

I was glad I had visited those ladies. They made me feel as though I was the same person I had always been. They certainly treated me the same.

On Sunday afternoon, I sat in the living room of my parent's home and looked out the window. The sun was shining brightly, and the daffodils blooming in the neighbor's yard were swaying in the breeze. I was thinking about Billy Joe and what he had said to me one time.

"Baby, no matter how bad life seems, it will always get better. But you must remember, no matter how good life seems, it will always get worse."

That day, I didn't think my life would ever be better. And I knew it couldn't get any worse. I couldn't imagine life without Billy Joe.

I had not told anyone what actually happened, except Phoebe and Al. I realized there was no one to tell, and I had nothing to say anyway. I wondered if I would have to keep it bottled up forever. There was not a single soul I could think of who wanted to hear about Billy Joe.

Mother acted nervous around me, and Daddy didn't speak to me at all.

I had spoken with Aunt Aggie once on the phone. Aunt Aggie said that Billy Joe had been restless since he was a teenager, and he couldn't settle down. I cried so much that I finally had to hang up. No matter what Aunt Aggie said to make me feel better, I still thought I had abandoned Billy Joe. I was afraid Aunt Aggie thought so, too.

I wondered what other people thought when they discovered I had moved back to Overton, but no one ever asked me why. Some people treated me as though I was in mourning. They acted fidgety and didn't know what to say to me. Even though I wanted to know what they were thinking, I didn't dare ask. Billy Joe would say that I worried too much about what people thought.

Billy Joe had worried about what people thought, too, regardless of what he said. I wondered if Billy Joe's life would have been different had he received counseling when he was a teenager. But people who had counseling in the 1950s were rejected by others and just as doomed as those sent to prison. I remembered Billy Joe telling me one time that feeling rejected was the worst feeling a person could have. I hoped Billy Joe realized that I had not rejected him; I had rejected his lifestyle.

Still deep in thought, I heard the phone ring. I got up from the sofa and stepped into the kitchen to answer it. The voice on the other end said, "Miss Moss, this is Billy Joe."

Three weeks had passed since Billy Joe had called me at work—three weeks since I had told him I could not see him anymore. I said, "Hi, Billy Joe."

He said, "I was wondering if I could get you to run me up to the train station in Atlanta. I have to catch a train, and I can't leave my car parked there. Will you pick me up at Aunt Aggie's in thirty minutes?"

I answered, "Okay."

Thirty minutes later, I pulled into Aunt Aggie's driveway. He came out to the car, opened the door and tossed his bag into the back seat. He got in, looked at me and said, "Hi, Baby."

I was happy to see him, but I didn't think I looked so happy. Driving was difficult; I was a little nervous. Billy Joe and I had not discussed my move. He had not explained his phone call the night he told me to go to Phoebe's for a week or two. Billy Joe wouldn't discuss what he called "history." And I had the good sense not to bring it up.

On the way to Atlanta, Billy Joe told me that he had to be in court the next morning. He said Matthew had to be there, too. The court case had something to do with when they were working together in Augusta and the surrounding area during the summer. Billy Joe said that diamonds were his business, not stocks and bonds. He said he wouldn't be going to court if he had stayed in his line of work.

I was thinking how glad I was that Billy Joe had destroyed the film in Sherry's camera at the pool that day in Augusta, or I could be going to court with them. That's when I realized that he had deliberately done it.

He told me he was taking the *Nancy Hanks* to Savannah, but he was getting off in Pembroke. He asked if I had ever ridden a train. I told him I took the *Nancy Hanks* from Macon to Columbus when I was in the fifth grade. He said he was taking the *Nancy Hanks II* and that the one I traveled on must have been her mama. We laughed.

We were nearing the train station when Billy Joe reached in his pocket and drew out a small black velvet pouch. As he placed it in my purse, he said, "Here are some diamonds. If anyone asks where they came from, just say they're from your uncle." I wondered if my suspicions concerning The Red Barn had been correct. I made no comment.

I turned into the parking lot at the train station. Tony's silver El Dorado pulled in next to my Mustang. Tony looked as sharp as a tack.

Billy Joe rolled down the window and said, "Tony, the last time I saw you, you looked like a bum. Now, here you are dressed like James Brown."

Tony smiled, waved at me and went into the train station.

Billy Joe turned and said, "Tony came to see me off."

I said, "Well, why didn't he pick you up?"

Billy Joe answered, "If he had picked me up, I would not have had a chance to see you, and I wanted to talk to you. I will probably never see you again after today. But here's the game plan. Go on with your life. You deserve to marry a good man and live happily ever after. I will not contact you. Don't wait for me; I won't be back this time, Jane.

"Remember me when you say your 'now I lay me down to sleep' prayers. But the most important thing is that, to your family, you have to act like I never existed. That's the only way you're going to make it with them. Can you do that for me?" He glanced away.

I had nothing to say. I could tell that Billy Joe didn't expect me to say anything. He wanted to do the talking. I knew that if I started talking before he had finished, he would place his index finger to his lips. I didn't want that happening.

Turning toward me again, looking me in the eye, Billy Joe said, "Needless to say, I will be very sad if you really forget about me. I know I will never forget you. I love you, Baby." He leaned over and kissed me on the forehead.

Then he opened the car door, got out, reached in the back seat and picked up his bag. He shut the door, turned and walked toward the train station entrance. I watched him go. He never looked back.

Epilogue

Mimi was right. Later on in life, my sister and I became good friends. She forgave me for not attending her wedding, but I never forgave myself. Jim was a good husband to Donna and a supportive brother-in-law to me. I had no children of my own. He and Donna shared theirs with me.

Al was right, and Daddy was right, too. I did come to a rude awakening. Al had warned me many times, but I didn't listen to him. Finally, I understood why Daddy didn't speak to me, and Milton Riggs acted the way he did toward me. They realized what was going on. Even though Daddy never mentioned anything to me, I should have listened to Milton Riggs.

In the late eighties and early nineties, all hell broke loose on the Gulf Coast. The so-called Dixie Mafia was in the news. Years later, there was a documentary citing the Gulf Coast corruption. I read that Mark and Colleen were divorced. Mark was sentenced to fifteen years in prison when he was in his sixties. His name was in the papers, and he was in the documentary that aired on television. I was dismayed. I couldn't believe such a nice person could be so bad.

Quite a few of Billy Joe's friends that I had met and with whom I had eaten breakfast, lunch and dinner were either dead or in prison. Billy Joe's name was in the news up to and including the year 1997. The papers were running old articles. They called him a "key member of the Dixie Mafia." Billy Joe would have said they used the words "Dixie Mafia" to sell papers. He had always told me there was no such thing as the Dixie Mafia. Even though I was not aware of anything of that magnitude, I was neither surprised nor disheartened.

Nothing could diminish my opinion of Billy Joe. I kept having visions of the game show where the master of ceremonies would say, "Will the real Billy Joe Billingsley please stand." The Billy Joe I knew would stand up each and every time.

I discovered that in 1968, Tony's bullet-riddled body had been found in Texas. He was said to be a Dixie Mafia pimp and burglar. Billy Joe had told me he was a pimp.

In 1970, Big Red's body was also found in Texas. He was described as a Dixie Mafia pimp, gambler, forger, and burglar. I had thought he was a bookie.

I learned that Jamie was an owner of one of the clubs when I read that he had been gunned down on "The Strip" in Biloxi. He had been delightful in Biloxi and in Vegas, and he liked my Mustang.

There was nothing in the papers concerning Harry Ledbetter. During the course of business, our paths crossed in 1972, but I had not seen him since. I spent a lot of time and money trying to locate him. I even looked at mug shots, thinking I would see his face with another name. I searched for Harry in the archives of newspapers and criminal records in Georgia, Texas, Oklahoma, Mississippi, Arkansas, Louisiana and Tennessee.

Harry had been operating a legitimate business in 1972, and I had realized then that there was no valid reason for my being afraid of him. I fully understood that not only had Billy Joe wanted me out of harm's way, so had Harry. I concluded that Harry must be out there somewhere, "walking the straight and narrow."

Fortunately, because of all my research into Harry's whereabouts, I did discover that there was no such thing as the "Dixie Mafia." The name was used in the South as a description for any and all criminals and people who did not have a "real" job. The "Dixie Mafia" included some law-abiding citizens and hardworking men and women who associated with those people. The term "Dixie Mafia" did not include all of the legitimate people who purchased and possessed stolen goods— people who were just as guilty as those who committed the crime.

Newspaper articles in a number of major cities throughout the southern states used the term "Dixie Mafia kingpin" to describe uneducated teenage punks, bootleggers, and college educated white-collar criminals. I failed to understand how all of those people with such conflicting aptitudes could be called "kingpin."

I learned that "Dixie Mafia" was a name made up by a law enforcement person and used by the news media to call attention to those who did not live within the boundaries of the law. There was no organization, and no one was in charge. Billy Joe had been right again, and I honestly believe he never lied to me.

Lucky, the greatest uncle in the whole world, was right when he said I was a survivor. He was familiar with everything that was going on. He tried to warn me, but Lucky recognized that I really was what he always called "hell-bent and determined."

All the people in my life have been right—except Blanche when she said, "Janie, you will forget, in time." On my visit to her in the hospital in 1990, Blanche told me that I had been very fortunate. I agreed with her. Blanche thought I was fortunate because I had moved back to Overton in 1968. I believed I was fortunate to have shared a small part of Billy Joe's life.

I told Blanche that sometimes I would undergo periods of intense thoughts of Billy Joe. That's when I would go out and buy expensive shoes. Purchasing as many as sixteen to twenty pairs in one year had cost me a small fortune. The awful truth was I didn't wear them; I collected them.

I brought Blanche up to date on what had happened in the past several years. I told her that Aunt Aggie had died, and in her will, she left the house to Tammy. I was invited to the housewarming after Tammy moved in.

I said, "Blanche, you know how silent I've been all these years about Billy Joe. When I arrived at the house, there was the 8x10 picture of Billy Joe and me that was taken in 1967 when we were in New Orleans. Over twenty years later, there it was—on the living room wall. Can you believe that?"

Blanche asked, "What did you do?"

I answered, "What could I do? All the ladies from the Baptist Church looked at it and said they thought I looked real pretty. Billy Joe had always been a mystery to them, but they would never utter an unkind word against him because of the Billingsley family. I noticed that they kept glancing at me and at each other. They would look up at the picture with an implication of 'I wish you'd look at that.' It reminded me of those two ladies in 1967 when I entered the elevator wearing a mini-dress."

A few months after the housewarming, Tammy called me and said she planned to sell the house. Since my livelihood at that time was real estate, she wanted to talk to me about it.

It seemed that another agent had told Tammy the house would bring an unbelievable top dollar price as commercial property. I told her it would be several years before she could get that price, even after it was re-zoned. She didn't want to wait, so she listed it with the other agent. That was okay with me. I didn't want a listing I couldn't sell.

When I told Blanche about the house, she asked me if it ever sold. I told her I didn't think so, and that I had thought of buying it myself. She asked, "Why would you want to do that?"

I said, "You know Billy Joe never lied to me. And he told me one time that he couldn't use a bank, so he had everything he owned stashed in the foundation of Aunt Aggie's house. There's no telling what's there. It could be money, diamonds, or both. I would have informed Tammy, but I didn't know how much she had been told about her dad. She probably still thinks he was that perfect man that I used to think he was. I guess the foundation of Aunt Aggie's house will end up no different than the attic of Lucky's Red Barn. I will never know what was there."

Phoebe and I are still friends. She retired several years ago, but she insists on working two or three days a week. She said, "I can't believe all that was written in the papers. Billy Joe was the perfect gentleman." And he was.

Billy Joe stayed in touch by phone, but that day at the train station was the last time I saw him. Shortly afterwards, he was in an auto accident. Many years later, I learned from an Attorney General's Intelligence Report that he was in possession of a large diamond at the time of the accident. My first reaction had been: "Why didn't you swallow it, Billy Joe?" But there was no need. Billy Joe died as a result of injuries sustained in that accident. The funeral was held at the Baptist Church. Billy Joe was also right when he said he would be in church again, "one day."

About the Author

Joan Moore Lewis, a native of Fayette County, Georgia, lived and worked in downtown Atlanta during the 1960s where she met a number of interesting and unusual people. She is a graduate of Southern Business University and attended Clayton State College. She is also a graduate of The Real Estate Academy and holds a Georgia Real Estate Associate Broker License.

At present, she is living and working in the Metro Atlanta area, and she spends weekends and holidays with family and friends. Her hobbies are collecting shoes and working on a second novel. *In His Corner* is her first published work.